THE VESPER BELL

PART I

By

J.B. Vosler

THE VESPER BELL

PART I

Sons of Jacob

Book VII

By

J.B. Vosler

The New Atlantian Library

ABSOLUTELY AMAZING eBOOKS

Manhanset House
Dering Harbor, New York 11965-0342

bricktower@aol.com ■ tech@absolutelyamazingebooks.com
■ absolutelyamazingebooks.com

Library of Congress Cataloging-in-Publication Data

Vosler, J.B.
The Vesper Bell, Part I
p. cm.

1. FICTION / Thrillers / Psychological
2. FICTION / Romance / Suspense
3. FICTION / Mystery & Detective / International Mystery &
Crime

ISBN: 978-1-955036-43-6, Trade Paper
Copyright © 2022, J.B. Vosler
Electronic compilation/ paperback edition
copyright © 2022 By Absolutely Amazing eBooks

October 2022

THE SONS OF JACOB Saga

BOOK I: *"Shadow of the Phoenix"*

This novel introduces MARTIN HENDERSON, who has survived a deadly fire only to return three-and-a-half years later as an assassin for EDWARD MORNINGSTAR, a Pentagon aide who sees himself as a Biblical Jacob. Henderson, once a brilliant entrepreneur, is now compelled to do whatever Morningstar asks – including murder – as a result of Morningstar's threat against a notable little girl, LILI PLATACIS. Henderson had sworn to protect Lili, and, when she is then taken, Henderson vows to bring down not only Morningstar, but his entire operation. In the meantime, Henderson's former lover, Senator Cynthia Madison – MADDI – has also become a Morningstar target, and it's up to Henderson to save her.

BOOK II: *"The Maker's Prophecy"*

The delusional Morningstar, who thinks he is Jacob, is well on his way to world domination. He has "adopted" twelve sons, who are his soldiers and will do whatever he asks. Henderson has made it his goal to stop Morningstar, and is doing what he can to undermine his efforts. Meanwhile, a deadly virus has been unleashed in Columbia, South Carolina, and Maddi's brother, ANDREW, as Medical Director of a downtown clinic, is the first to see its effects. When a more aggressive strain of the same virus shows up in Chicago, L.A., and Texas, Henderson knows Morningstar is somehow behind it. Maddi is once again threatened, and he must figure out a way to keep her safe from Morningstar's relentless pursuit.

BOOK III: *"The Rise of the Avenger"*

An entire village is massacred outside the town of Bariloche, Argentina, and Maddi is pulled into action at the request of one of her dearest friends, SIR ARTHUR KAUFFOLD, a former ambassador. She puts together a coalition to travel to the region. Morningstar learns of it, and sends two 'sons' to Bariloche to stop her. She succeeds not only in defending the coalition, but in averting a war with Argentina, thanks to the intervention of her former lover, HANK CLARKSON, the Deputy Director of Homeland Security. Meanwhile, Henderson has gone to Russia to undergo a revolutionary surgery designed to give him a completely new face. He then vows to seek revenge against Morningstar.

BOOK IV: *"Strike of the Cobra"*

A vicious assassin, COBRA, has killed a former IRA operative outside Donegal, which has thrown the Irish Republic into chaos. Cobra, also known as Dan, is one of the sons of Jacob, and has been instructed by Morningstar to carry out multiple killings in an effort to disrupt the UK and France. Maddi discovers that she is being stalked by someone from the UK, and insists on flying to London to find him. Henderson, who has undergone surgery and has changed his name to MATT, goes to D.C. to introduce himself to Maddi as Martin's cousin. He learns she has gone to the UK, and – when he learns why – follows her there. Hank does the same, and the two men are forced to work together to keep her safe.

BOOK V: *"A Battle for Justice"*

MARK JUSTICE, a British Private Inquiry Agent, seeks help for debilitating headaches, only to learn that he has an evil alter ego. Maddi had sought his help to find her stalker, and he has now become obsessed with her. She has left London to meet up with Henderson at his Latvian estate, their first reunion after four long, desperate years. Hank follows them, but then sees Maddi's devotion to Henderson, and decides to leave. But before he can, he learns that his CIA agent son, ROGER CLARKSON, has been taken by Cobra. He and Henderson are again forced to work together to try to not only keep Maddi safe from Morningstar, but to find Roger and save him from Cobra. It is then that Hank learns a terrible secret about Henderson.

BOOK VI: *"The Morning Star"*

A Nazi-era warship has been under the protection of a small group of families since its discovery in the late 1940's. Calling themselves "The Morning Star," a translation of the vessel's name, the group's mission is twofold: to understand its technology, and to keep it from falling into the wrong hands. When a powerful neo-Nazi threatens them and tries to steal the warship, the group is called into action. Led by Henderson's father, WALTER, they must do all they can to protect the vessel. Morningstar learns of the group, and assigns his son, SIMEON, to infiltrate their organization, which is about to meet in Paris. Meanwhile, Henderson and Hank arrive in Paris to save Roger from Cobra, and are led on a deadly game of cat-and-mouse. Maddi follows them, and saves Roger, but is devastated to learn that Henderson has been taken by the infamous killer.

"I go, and it is done;
the bell invites me."
"Hear it not, Duncan, for it is a knell
That summons thee
to heaven or to hell."

~ William Shakespeare, Macbeth ~

Prologue

Am I dead? The words flashed in Lili's mind like fireflies on a warm summer night. It was the first thought she had had in quite a while. And it reassured her. After all, if she was thinking, she couldn't be dead...right? She tried to open her eyes. It hurt, so she only opened them partway. All she saw were shadows from moonlight outside a window, and a faint spot of light in the distant sky. She focused on the light. *What is it?* Out of nowhere, she heard a voice say, *"It's the morning star, Lili. It can guide you...or kill you."*

Her eyes flew open. *Who said that?* She tried to see around her; she couldn't, but sensed no one else in the room. She turned again to the window. The light in the distance had grown brighter; more distinct. "The morning star," she whispered, then sat up, startled. It was strange to hear her own voice, even as a whisper. She looked again, unsure why she had become so fixated on the yellow-white light that hung in the sky like a sun or a moon...or the eye of a coal-black raven.

The morning star. Lili had read about the morning star, but had never quite understood it. It seemed to represent so many things. Some swore it was the star of Lucifer, while others insisted that it symbolized triumph over sin...the promise of God and eternal life. Something evil or something good...scholars were clearly divided. Lili felt it to be neither, knowing it only as the planet Venus, visible in the east in the early morning sky just before sunrise.

She continued to stare, imagining a planet rotating around the sun millions of miles away. The longer she looked, the more she could see other features of the night sky.

i

Shadows over hillsides; starlight over trees. *Where am I?* She tried to move; she couldn't. It was as if her arms were tied to imaginary posts. She looked down; she wasn't tied to anything. But she may as well have been...she was too weak to move. *How long have I been here?* She closed her eyes, trying to remember...she couldn't.

Suddenly she shivered as she saw an image of herself lying still in a snow-covered field. Her eyes were closed, her arms crossed on her chest, and she was cold...so cold. The question came again. *Am I dead?* Was that image real...was it her...was she dead? She forced her eyes open and looked again at the dark sky and the bright light, and was comforted. If she was staring at a star, then she couldn't be dead...right? But what if she was dead, and the light in the distance wasn't Venus, but was that light that so many claimed to see when they died but were not yet gone? What if it represented a call to heaven...or a warning from hell?

She felt a shudder run through her, and again tried to move her arms. She was able to lift her right hand, but it took all of her strength. She looked at it, sticklike in the shadows, and was stunned at how thin and weak it had become. She moved her fingers; they looked like tiny branches swaying in the wind as even the simplest movement sent pain up and down her arm. She tried to recall what had happened...where she had been before she had lost all recollection of time.

Ventspils...I was at Danil's house in Ventspils. Danil Latkovskis, a friend of her father's, had cared for her after her father was killed. Her mother had died the year before, and the man who had initially promised to look after her – Martin Henderson – had died in a hotel fire just days after her father's death. Only five years old at the time, she had felt so frightened and alone, but Danil and his sister, Anna had taken her in. They had made her feel welcome; they had made her feel at home.

She felt a catch in her throat. She missed them...their laughs, the breakfasts in the big kitchen, the frost on her bedroom window...but mostly she missed the cats. It had been her job to take care of them, and she found herself worried for them. Surely Danil was feeding them and giving them water...wasn't he? She nodded, the effort causing a pain to shoot up the back of her neck. She put her hand to it and rubbed, stunned at the feel of her cold skin under her fingers.

She took a deep breath, and – with great effort – managed to sit up straight. She looked around the room, able to see it more clearly now that the light in the distance had grown brighter. The room was small, with only the bed that she was sitting on, a dresser, a lamp, and an open closet. There were two dresses hanging in the closet, but she couldn't tell what color they were. They looked like skinny shadow-people hanging from a rod. Again, she shivered.

She shifted on the bed, then stretched her legs, stifling a cry as the muscles rebelled against the movement. But she kept them stretched, then shook them, trying to get them to do what they used to do without her having to think about it. After a minute or two, she was able to bend them and tuck them underneath her. She sat on her heels, put her hands on the window sill, and pulled herself up so she could get a better look at the star in the distance. It had brightened even more, making the sky around it seem darker. Beyond it she could see a glimmer of sunrise...a faint band of yellow barely visible over the highest ridge of the mountains. It was clear now that she was nowhere near Ventspils. The mountains she was looking at were taller than any she had ever seen in Latvia, with far more rocks and far fewer trees. They looked colder, too. But mostly they were taller, and they loomed over her like a giant Saskatchewan, the oversized man/beast that she had read about in her science books.

She focused again on the light in the distance. *The morning star.* Lili's mother had spoken often of the star. She had told Lili that it would be important someday...that there would come a time when the preservation of everything that she knew and loved and cared about would be reliant on the rise – or fall – of that star.

Out of nowhere, images entered her mind...faces of men she had never met, with dark eyes and darker souls that she could only feel. Their names streamed across her consciousness as if on a marquee...Adolf, Edward, Mark. She saw maps of places she recognized...Latvia, Germany, Indonesia; as if she was thumbing through an atlas or an encyclopedia. *Who are these men, these places...and why are they important?*

A wind squall gusted against the window and caused it to shake; she could feel cold air through the glass. She grabbed the coverlet from the bed and went to pull it over her shoulders, when she heard something fall to the floor. She froze. Slowly, she crept backward and slid off the side of the bed. She tried to stand; her legs buckled; they couldn't hold her. She fell to the floor, pulling the coverlet down with her. She looked over and spotted the item that had fallen...it was a sketchpad. She reached for the oversized pad; the front cover was blank. She opened it and, using the moonlight, was able to see page after page of drawings; sketches of places and people...some she recognized, some she didn't. *Who are they? Where are they?* Had she made the sketches? The more she looked, the more she knew that she had.

She thumbed through the pages, stopping when she came to a familiar face. She choked. *Uncle Mart.* Though he had been killed years ago in a fire, she had continued to feel his presence inside her. And it made sense. Mart had been a vital part of her world. A member of a highly respected family that lived in a castle not far from her home, he had been every bit the uncle she had called him, though they shared no blood ties at all. Her eyes began to burn, and she rubbed them.

She turned the page. There was a sketch of a castle – the Henderson castle – and next to it were drawings of Walter and Dora, Mart's papa and mama. Lili angled the pad to take in more of the moonlight. She had captured them well; Walter with his dark hair, light eyes and easy smile, and Dora with her lovely gold hair and even lighter eyes. Lili felt a lump in her throat. The Hendersons had been kind to her and her family; it was painful to see them again, even if it was just in sketches on a page.

The next drawing was of a church, and she felt a sudden uneasiness as she looked at a six-sided star hanging over the door. She frowned as she tried to think what might have made her draw the church or the star. She didn't know; she couldn't recall ever seeing either one. She had sketched mountains in the background, similar to the ones outside her window, though she had covered them in trees. Above the drawing she had written "Where good and bad exist as one." She flinched. *What does that mean?*

Next was a drawing of Danil...the brave freedom fighter who had cared for her after her parents and Mart were gone. He was wearing the eye patch that he had been wearing when she had seen him last...the result of an injury from the same explosion that had killed her father. She fought tears. *I miss you, Danil.*

She flipped to the next page and gasped, covering her mouth as feelings of dread consumed her. The page was covered in black crayon, and specks of dark wax were flaking to the floor. Within the black were three white circles the size of cotton balls; they looked like clouds. In the first circle was a bold red swastika. Just seeing it – and imagining herself drawing it – made her feel sick inside. The second circle had a sketch of a snake...a cobra by the way it was hooding its neck.

The third circle held an image of a star, not the six-sided one; it was brighter and less distinct...more like the morning star that had begun to fade in the distance. *What does it mean?* she wondered, *and why did I draw these three things on a page of all black?*

She flipped to the next page and her dread turned to panic. Splattered with orange and yellow crayon, it was clearly a fire. Was it the fire that had killed Uncle Mart? She looked closer. No, it was coming from the earth...an earthquake? A volcano? There were palm trees and maples, and lots of blue water surrounding it all.

She hurriedly turned the page, and was met with a collage of sketches. The first was a brown book that looked like a diary. On the cover, written in German, were the words "Er allein, dem die Jugend gehört, gewinnt die Zukunft." *He alone, who owns the youth, gains the future.* Beside it was drawn a series of constellations; straight lines between dark blue stars with a gray background. There were seven of them, and she recognized three; the Big Dipper, Orion, Vulpecula. Below the constellations was a sketch of an oval-shaped gemstone. It was boldly blue, evident even in the moonlight, and it seemed familiar, though she couldn't recall ever seeing such a stone. It was surrounded by seven copper-colored circles...coins? They were bigger than the gemstone, but far less distinct. Finally, in the lower righthand corner was what looked like an airship...a flying saucer of sorts. Her breathing had become shallow and her heart was racing. *What does all of this mean?* She trembled, overcome by the sketches that her very own hands had drawn.

She turned the page, and saw a drawing of a young boy. Her eyes filled with tears. *Ricardo.* Though she had never met him, she had somehow connected with him after a most horrid event...the massacre of his entire Argentine village. She had reached out to comfort him, and had then asked him to give a message to a woman she had also never met, but felt as if she had known all her life. *Mart's special lady.*

> *"Tell her to forgive him...he only did it to keep me safe."*

Had Ricardo given her the message? Lili sighed. She prayed that he had. A bigger question: *Had the special lady understood?*

On the next page was a sketch of that lady. High cheekbones, blond hair to her shoulders; she was lovely. She, too, looked familiar, though the two had never met. Lili knew that if ever the day was to come when they did meet, they would be fast friends. But, like Lili in the snow, the woman was lying still in a forest, her eyes closed. *Is she dead, too?* came a thought out of nowhere. Lili shook her head quickly. *Dear God...don't let her be dead.*

She flipped to the next page. It was blank, but for a single word.

Justice

Lili shook her head, confused. She understood the word justice, but she couldn't imagine why she would have written only that word on a page of the tablet.

She was about to turn to the next page, when she heard a door close somewhere far away, followed by the tapping of footsteps. She closed the tablet, shoved it under the mattress, then grabbed the coverlet. She threw it on the bed, struggled up herself, then slid underneath it, unsure who – or what – might be coming down the hall. As she lay there shivering, her teeth chattering, she thought to herself, *I'm definitely not dead...yet.*

DAY I

"When spider webs unite, they can tie up a lion."

~ African proverb ~

MONDAY, MARCH 15ᵀᴴ, 2004

CHAPTER 1

Paris, France

"How soon can I book a train to Lyon?" Walter Henderson was gripping the phone as he leaned on the desk and spoke to the concierge in a crisp French dialect.

"Are you referring to the TGV?" the man asked, also in French.

"Yes," Walter replied, knowing high-speed rail was the quickest way to Lyon.

"It leaves every hour, sir, starting at 6:30 in the morning. If you are ready now, I could get you on the 9:30 train."

Walter checked his watch. *9:00.* "Perfect. I'll need a car to the station." He paused. "But I'd like to keep the room. If things go as planned, I'll be back tonight."

"Oui, Monsieur."

Walter hung up the phone. He had been pacing his Paris hotel suite for the last half-hour, unsure what to do. The text he had received minutes ago had totally unnerved him. It was from the infamous Cobra, an assassin...who was also his son. He pulled out his cellphone and stared down at the text.

"The party begins at Place Bellecour...our favorite hangout, Pops. Bring your lovely wife, Dora. You can use the family jet. Be there by this afternoon."

He threw the phone on the desk. 'The party' Cobra was referring to included Walter's nephew, Matt, whom Walter had become aware of just two weeks ago. But in that short time, Matt had proven his worth, risking his own safety to keep those at the Henderson castle safe from an intruder.

1

Reassured by the act, Walter had invited Matt to a meeting in Paris, which consisted of a handful of heirs that were privy to a secret. That secret involved a remarkable but deadly warship, known as *Der Morgenstern.*

When Matt didn't show, Walter had tried to call him. The call had been answered by Cobra, who had informed Walter that he had kidnapped Matt, and was planning a party, *"...for the whole family."* The text had come minutes later, inviting not only Walter, but his wife, Dora, to Lyon.

But Walter was in Paris, expected to deliver a noon lecture to attendees of the NATO conference. He had been asked by the President himself to give that lecture; he couldn't just skip it. But he also couldn't just sit in his hotel suite for the next three hours waiting to give the lecture while his nephew was in the grips of the Cobra.

Cobra had assumed that Walter was at his home in Boston. But even if Walter had left Boston the second that he received Cobra's text, he would have been pushing it to get to Lyon by late afternoon. Which gave Walter an advantage. If he could get to Place Bellecour hours before Cobra expected him, maybe he could find Cobra, catch him off guard, and save his nephew, Matt. It was worth a try.

He pulled a pen and a pad of paper from a drawer of the desk and jotted a quick note explaining that he had been called away unexpectedly. He folded it and stuffed it in his pocket. He would have the concierge deliver it to those overseeing the lectures. That should be enough to keep them from looking for him.

But it wasn't the lecture committee – or even the U.S. President – that had him worried. No, it was a group that he had been a member of for most of his adult life. Known as the Morning Star – the English translation of *Der Morgenstern* – it was that group that had brought him to Paris in the first place. They had called a meeting, the first in eight years, due to a threat from a German neo-Nazi, Adolf Mueller. He had vowed to steal the vessel the group had been tasked with protecting, and they had met to try to stop him. The meeting had started at ten the night before, and hadn't ended until eight the following morning...about an hour ago. Things had not gone well. The group's leader, Sean MacPherson, had chosen to fight alongside his army to protect the ship. He was killed, the warship they had hidden for six decades was taken, and the man who stole it, Mueller, had died, too, leaving them with no way to know the location of the warship, or if it was even still in one piece. Though the Morning Star soldiers had succeeded in killing Mueller's army, they had been destroyed, as well, which left the group with no leader, no army, no ship. They had elected to go to their rooms and rest, with a plan to regroup after Walter's lecture.

He frowned. If he chose to go to Lyon now, not only would he miss his lecture, but he would miss their meeting, which would alarm the others. Should he tell them? Maybe call Kauffold and let him know? He sighed. *No, he'll ask too many questions. No one can know of Cobra, least of all the members of the Morning Star.*

He walked to the window and looked outside. It was March, which meant that spring was close. He could see its promise in the buds on a few of the trees, and in the row of daffodils that lined the walkway beneath his Paris hotel room. He cracked the window and breathed in the morning air. It smelled clean and fresh. He sighed. It was deceiving. Spring didn't feel close at all.

He closed the window and walked back to the desk.

He combed his fingers through silver-gray hair, his six-four frame weary, even a bit stooped. Suddenly, he felt all of his 72 years. He picked up his cellphone and looked again at Cobra's text. Shouldn't he alert someone? The police? Or maybe Interpol? The international police force had been looking for Cobra for the past decade, his murders spanning at least five continents. Walter knew they would give anything for a lead. *How many lives might be saved?*

He flinched. Again, he threw the phone on the desk. In spite of the good it might do – the people it might save – he couldn't tell the police; he couldn't tell anyone. To do so could put his nephew at risk. Who knew what Cobra might do to Matt if he saw a team of officers coming for him. The truth was that he didn't *want* to tell the police, because then he would have to explain how he knew Cobra; what it was that tied the two men to one another. *Why that brutal killer calls me father.*

He grimaced. He thought of his wife, Dora. What should he do about her? Cobra had insisted that he bring her to the so-called party, but there was no way in hell he would ask Dora to join him. Not only would it put her in danger, but his wife knew nothing of his lovechild, Cobra. *And she never will.* But what would Cobra do if Walter showed up without her? He bristled. *He won't care. It's me he wants.*

He took off his suit coat, hung it on a chair, and walked into the bathroom. He splashed water on his face, then stared at eyes that looked so much like his son's; not Cobra, but Martin...the good son. Martin had been the consummate Henderson heir, the promising successor that had been born to his wife, Dora, not his mistress, Nenita. But Martin was gone, lost in a fire years ago, which had left Cobra as the only true heir...until Matt came along. But now, Matt's life was in danger...because of Cobra.

Walter dried his face and sighed. *What a mess you've made, Walter.*

He walked out of the bathroom, put on his jacket, and opened the closet. He stared at his clothes; two suits and an extra pair of shoes. He would leave them there...as a promise to himself that he would come back soon.

4

He picked up a stack of papers from the desk. Left to him by his father, those papers consisted of page after page of astral constellations. Jeremy Henderson had researched the constellations over the course of nearly forty years, and had copied them – one by one – onto each of those pages. They were pivotal to the Morning Star mission, though Walter had no idea how. He slid them into his briefcase and locked it, first with a numerical code, then with his fingerprint. The case, given to him by his father, Jeremy, had a unique design. Smaller than most, it was brown leather with black leather trim. The letters JH were etched in the side. He had given it to Walter when he joined the Morning Star. *"How will it recognize my fingerprint?"* Walter had asked. His father had smiled, his kind blue eyes reassuring, as they had always been.

"It only needs for you to be a Henderson." Walter frowned as he stared at the case. Should he bring it with him, or lock it in the safe? *I was told to keep these sketches either with me or in Boston.* He sighed and threw the strap over his shoulder.

He picked up his cellphone and reread the text. He slid the phone in his pocket. He would keep the briefcase and the phone with him at all times. The briefcase held the drawings that were vital to the secret of the Morning Star. The cellphone held a text that was vital to the secret of Walter's role in the making of a killer. It was imperative that the world never learn of either one. He sighed and left the suite. *Here I come, Matt, to try to save you from...my son*

.

CHAPTER 2

Somewhere over the Philippines

Psychiatrist James Samuels put his hand on his stomach as he looked out the window of the prop plane, watching it come to a landing in a way-too-small airstrip outside Baclayon in the Philippines. The last leg of the journey had been a tough one, his poor gut jostled by the small plane's flight from Manila. Though he might have liked to have viewed this trip as a much-needed vacation, it was far from it. Not only had he traveled too far without the comforts he would've preferred, but he had come on a mission...a journey of discovery. His goal: to learn more about his recent client, Mark Justice, and how he had come to be. The fact that Justice was the alter ego to a killer had only added to Samuels' curiosity, and he had decided that his quest would be best-served by gaining an understanding of the boy, Mark Villamor, from which the two egos had emerged. It was fascinating to think that a child's ill-fated destiny at a boarding school had demanded the creation of not just one protector, but two.

Samuels checked his watch. Still set to British time, it said 9:00 a.m. As he looked out the window, it was clear that the sun wasn't rising, but would soon begin to set, and he changed his watch accordingly. *Go forward seven hours, Samuels.* That seven hours would wreak havoc on his internal clock, but there was nothing to do about it; this trip was necessary. After all, it was because of Samuels that the killer, Cobra, was once again on the loose. Samuels had been the psychiatrist whom Mark Justice had turned to in an effort to uncover the cause of debilitating headaches. After the first visit, Samuels had begun to grasp the implausible truth: the

7

refined Justice was also the infamous Cobra; they were one and the same. Justice himself had come to that same realization a few days later; that was when everything had gone to hell. Repulsed by it, Justice had run from Samuels before he could alert the authorities.

Samuels flinched. That wasn't exactly true. Samuels had hesitated calling the authorities, battling his need to hold onto the most amazing case of disassociation he had ever seen. The guilt from that hapless delay had yet to ease, which was another reason for the journey. Samuels had to somehow make things right.

The discovery that the two men inhabited the same body had been staggering. Justice, a distinguished investigator, was a gentle, well-dressed man with fair skin, blond hair, and kind blue eyes, while Cobra was anything but. Disheveled and dressed all in black, with stringy dark hair that hung to his shoulders, he was unkempt in body and soul. No two men could be more different, yet, there they were, Justice and Cobra, two divergent souls in the very same man. *Dissociative Identity Disorder* it was called in the psychiatric community; "split personality," to the layman. Its very existence was challenged by most psychiatrists, but there had been no denying it, and Samuels had been eager to delve into the case, not only for his own enlightenment, but to finally silence his many critics who saw him as a relic from the past. His fascination with Freud was from a bygone era, and Samuels had suffered the slings and arrows of his colleagues for the past fifty years. Finally, he had proof of Freud's unique take on the Id and the Ego, and had hoped that Justice would go willingly to a mental facility – which Samuels had told him was a spa – where Samuels could study and document the disorder, and help the poor man at the same time. Though Justice had agreed to go, he must have seen through the ruse, and had cleverly evaded Samuels by way of a bathroom window. He had then resumed his identity as Cobra, and had killed again. Samuels grimaced. *Which puts that blood on my hands.*

Once he had realized that Justice had fled, he had tried to call the Chief Inspector of Scotland Yard, Sir Lionel Pritchard. But the Inspector had been out of town, and Samuels hadn't been comfortable leaving the information with a subordinate. So, he had agreed to call back Monday, which was today, but in the meantime had decided to make the trip to Baclayon. He had tried to call before he left, then during his layover in Amsterdam, and finally during his most recent stop in Manila. All three times, he was told the man was still out of town. Frustrated, he had insisted the Yard have Pritchard call him the minute he got back. So far, he had received no call.

He had spent the rest of Friday, all of Saturday, and Sunday morning searching for Justice, first at the man's office in Belgrave Square, then in the park where he had gone for refuge when he had discovered his tie to Cobra. Samuels had even journeyed to the East End to look for him at the site of Cobra's recent murder of the brave paramedic, Cora Winslow, whose nametag Justice had shown to Samuels that first day they met. When Samuels had tried to take the nametag, Justice had made a point of holding on to it, which made Samuels think that maybe Cora's murder held special meaning. But Justice had been in none of those places, which had left Samuels with nowhere else to look. That was when he had decided that his best hope to find Justice – and Cobra – was to travel to where the child, Mark, had been born. The journey had been a long one, starting at London's Heathrow Airport, with stops in Amsterdam and Manila, ending twenty hours later at the small airfield near Baclayon.

It was late afternoon in the Philippines, and, as Samuels prepared to leave the plane, he guessed it would be hot. He had left a cool, misty London afternoon, and was wearing a somewhat heavy wool jacket. He took it off and draped it over his arm, then slung his satchel – his only piece of luggage – over his shoulder. He walked out the door of the plane and was met instantly with smothering heat. He followed the other passengers down a flight of stairs and across the tarmac, taking a handkerchief from his vest pocket and wiping his forehead as beads of sweat instantly appeared. Hot didn't begin to describe the stifling air, and, as he walked to the front of the terminal in search of a taxi, all he could hope was that the cab had air-conditioning.

He had decided his first stop would be the boarding school where, from what he had learned from Justice, the alter ego Cobra had been created. Mark Villamor, an already troubled boy, had been sent to the school for discipline. Once there, he had been abused by the headmaster, and his only salvation had come with the creation of the monster, Cobra. It seemed odd that a savior would assume the guise of a killer. Did it take a cruel assassin to save a defenseless little boy? Samuels sighed. *Perhaps.*

Justice hadn't told him the name of the boarding school, and, as he waited for a cab, he hoped there was only one. A taxi pulled up and he slid in back. "The boarding school," he said matter-of-factly, hoping his English would be understood.

The brown-skinned cabby nodded and left the terminal. Samuels' hope for air-conditioning wasn't to be, and he rolled down the window to let air into the sweltering cab. It was one of the few times where he wished he didn't have a beard. As he looked out, he noted that Baclayon was as opposite from London as anything could be. The heat seemed to emanate from the pavement like waves of mist from the underworld, and the air – though damp like London – was sticky and hot instead of foggy and cool. There wasn't a soul in sight, and only a smattering of one-story buildings dotted the landscape. He sighed. To think; it was on these tarred and steamy streets that the boy, Mark Villamor, had been transformed into a brutal killer. How? Why? What went wrong? Why can one man suffer unbearable anguish and keep his sanity, while another loses himself entirely? Samuels had devoted his life to solving that mystery. Forty years later he still didn't have an answer.

The streets soon became rough dirt roads and Samuels again put a hand on his stomach. He was starting to feel queasy, and, just as he thought he might need to have the driver stop, the man pulled into a parking lot in front of an odd-looking, one-story building. The layout was in the shape of a boomerang; a central area with an angled wing to each side. It had been constructed with white siding, which was now a faded gray, and the roof consisted of red metal slats angled forward and back. He frowned. Where had he seen that same design? He nodded. *Scotland...in some of the low-lying moors.* He couldn't identify the architecture, but knew that it dated back well before the twentieth century. He looked at the aging columns and the discolored metal doors; whenever it had been built, it appeared that only basic maintenance had been done since. He spotted a sign, "Baclayon boarding school, founded in 1762." It was posted directly in front of a life-size statue of Dawsonne Drake. Samuels shook his head and sighed. *Of course...a British colonizer was behind the building of this school.*

He paid the driver and stepped out of the cab. "Could you please wait, sir?"

The driver nodded and Samuels approached the statue...an armored man on horseback; a sword in one hand, a gun in the other. The soldier was outfitted in the apparel of a 1700's British merchant. Etched in stone beneath the statue were the words, "The Governor of Manila, on behalf of His Majesty, the King."

Samuels walked past the statue toward the school. He stepped on what had once been a stone walkway, placing his feet carefully to avoid stumbling over clumps of grass amid broken stones. As he reached the front entrance, he again noted the building's age. A crack in the wall had been painted over, and the front door could use a coat of paint. He climbed a set of stairs and put his hand on the knob. He hesitated, oddly uneasy. *You've come a long way, Samuels, now get on with it.* He opened the door and stepped inside. He was greeted with odors of the past. The not-so-unpleasant scent of old books, mixed with the dank smells of a bygone era. The tile was faded, the woodwork pocked; the place clearly hadn't been remodeled in a very long time. The only exception was the wing to the right. It looked newer than the rest; as if it had been rebuilt within the last ten years or so; newer walls, modern fixtures on the doors and windows. *Why was only one wing remodeled?*

There were no students in the hallways, and he checked his watch. *4:50 p.m.* He guessed they had gone to their rooms to prepare for dinner. He searched for an office. *Will someone still be working?* He found a room with a sign by a closed door which said '*Opisina.*' He didn't know what that meant, but the room had the look and feel of an office. He walked in, heartened to see an older woman with dark skin and high cheekbones shuffling through papers on her desk. She looked up, lowered a pair of reading glasses, and smiled. "Maaari ba kitang tulungan?"

Samuels frowned. "I'm sorry Madam, but I only speak English."

The woman nodded. With a pleasant accent, she said, "How may I help?"

"I'm looking for information. I'd like to know about a boy who went to this school about fifteen years ago."

The woman frowned. "And you are?"

Samuels pulled out his ID and held it up for her. "Dr. James Samuels. I'm the man's doctor and I need a bit of background information in order to help him."

She studied the ID, then stared at Samuels. He shifted uncomfortably. Finally, she nodded. "I will check files. His name?"

"Mark Villamor."

"One moment, please."

She stood and walked to a metal cabinet. She knelt down, opened a drawer, and rifled through folders, finally pulling out a faded yellow file. "Here it is. I am surprised we have this after so many years...especially after the fire." She stood, walked to her desk, and laid down the file. "What do you want to know?"

What do I want to know? Everything. "Whatever you can tell me, actually."

The woman opened the file, skimmed through several pages, and nodded. "He attended this school from age twelve to sixteen. He was bright, but often in trouble, especially toward the end." She turned a page, then gasped. "Oh dear."

"What? What is it?"

"He was let go. A fight with the headmaster."

Samuels nodded, not surprised. *And in comes Cobra.* "Does it list an address where his family lived?"

She returned to the front of the file. "He lived with his mother in a small village about thirty miles south of here...on route seven. Twelve Conquistador."

Samuels had pulled a pad from his travel bag and wrote down the information. He stuffed the pad in his pocket and reached out his hand. "Thank you, Madam."

She shook his hand. "Glad to be of help, Doctor."

He turned to leave, then spun around to face her. "One more thing."

"Yes?"

"You don't happen to have a picture of him, do you?"

She flipped to the last page of the file. She removed a small polaroid from a pocket in the file and held it up for him to see. "It is not so clear after all this time."

He pulled reading glasses from his pocket. The photo was small, and she was right; the colors had faded and the resolution was poor. But Samuels saw what he needed to see. As he stared at the picture, he felt his blood run cold. He had always believed the adage that the eyes were the window to the soul. Clearly, Mark Villamor was no exception.

He returned his glasses to his vest, thanked the woman, and left the school. He walked out to the waiting cab, surprised to find that he was shaking. He climbed in back and gave the man the address for Mrs. Villamor, hoping, by some stroke of luck, she was still there. He leaned back, taking deep breaths in an effort to calm down. He saw the picture of the boy in his mind and shivered anew. Yes, it was true; the eyes were the window to the soul. *Two different eyes...two different souls.*

CHAPTER 3

Paris, France

Secret Service agent Spencer Seacroft handed the train attendant tickets for the three of them: himself, a second agent, Nigel Brooks, and their protectee, Senator Cynthia Madison. The clerk put a checkmark on each voucher, then handed them back and moved further down the aisle. Seacroft slid the vouchers in his pocket as he looked at the senator. She was asleep, her head on the arm of the seat. He yawned as he tried to keep his own eyes open. None of them had had a decent night's sleep in over a week; they were all feeling it, but none more than Seacroft.

When he had been given the assignment of protecting Madison, the well-known senator from Indiana, he had been heartened. He had met her several times while serving as an agent for the prior administration's Vice-president, and knew her to be a delightful, engaging woman. Little did he know that she would take him on a whirlwind journey from London to Lyon, with stops in Latvia and Paris along the way. There had been several attempts on her life during that time, and it was only by luck – and the intervention of Matt Henderson – that she wasn't dead.

The second agent, Nigel Brooks, had come aboard in London, soon after the tragedies at the Queen's Ball. One of the senator's agents had needed to return to the U.S., and Inspector Pritchard, still stinging from the murder of America's Secretary of State and the poisoning of a U.S. Senator – both occurring at the Ball – had offered the highly-skilled Brooks to replace him. Brooks had been a good addition, adjusting quickly to the lifestyle of the bold and daring Madison. And he hadn't complained, not once. Even his sprained ankle from climbing the gate at the Hendersons' Latvian compound three days ago hadn't brought a word of protest. They had scaled the gate thinking they were rescuing Maddi, but as Seacroft looked back on it now, she was actually safer at that estate than anywhere else on earth. *So why did we leave?*

Maddi – a nickname that only her closest friends were aware of – had gone to the compound in search of Matt Henderson, though Seacroft hadn't understood why at the time. Then he had seen the goodbye between them, and he knew: she was in love with the man. Which was really none of his business, except that the relationship continued to put her in danger. Were it not for Matt, she and Seacroft would be comfortably back in DC, and all he would have to worry about were snipers or tainted letters. Now he had an entire world to worry about. It didn't help that she was so calm about the whole thing. *"I'll be fine, Seacroft,"* she would always say. *"I have you to protect me."* Then she would grin and he would be completely lost for a reply.

So far, he had managed to keep her safe, but he knew his luck would run out sooner or later. He had tried to convince her that they should return home and let the authorities go in search of Matt, but she had vehemently refused, saying, *"There are things you don't know, Spencer. We could jeopardize so much if we call in the police."* She had added, *"He saved my life, and Roger's life. Now it's time we return the favor."* The point was hard to argue; the man *had* saved her life, more than once. And he had saved Roger Clarkson's life, as well. The CIA agent, who just happened to be the son of Maddi's former boyfriend, Hank, had been kidnapped by Cobra and, from what Seacroft could gather, Matt had persuaded Cobra to leave Roger and take him instead. As a result, they were on their way to Lyon...to save Matt. Maddi had gotten a text a few hours ago saying that he had escaped and was waiting for her *"...at Place Bellecour."* Seacroft had been wary; anyone could have written it. But, after another quick text, she had assured him it was Matt. *"We share a secret, Spencer. Trust me, it's him."*

Seacroft stretched his long legs in front of him as he looked at Maddi and sighed. She found ways to get into trouble that would have stymied the cleverest of agents. He felt like he was always playing catch-up rather than serving the intended role of anticipating and protecting. But it was worth it; she was one of the finest individuals he had ever looked after, and, though she had put him and Brooks through hell, she had earned his devotion. He would do whatever he could to keep her safe.

He yawned and rubbed his eyes. He needed to sleep. But he knew it would be futile. His mind was busy reviewing all that had to be done to prepare for Lyon. The train ride would take about two and a half hours, which would put them in the city around one p.m., local time. *Seven in the morning in the U.S.* He hadn't spoken to his boss, Sam Allen, since six a.m. EST, which was about five hours ago. He was expected to call him every six hours, which would put the next call at noon, but they would still be on the train. There was nowhere on the train that was private enough for such a call, which meant that he would have to wait until they got to Lyon. The call would be an hour or so late, but he guessed that Allen was used to that, by now. After all, Seacroft was looking after the unpredictable Cynthia Madison.

His stomach growled. *How can I be hungry?* They had been delayed in Paris by a bus accident not far from the hospital and had missed the nine-thirty train. So, they had decided to get breakfast while they waited for the next train at ten-thirty. But not one of them had eaten more than a few bites, their appetites curbed by all that had taken place since they had left DC two weeks ago.

He shook his head and sighed. It was hard to believe that so much had happened in only two weeks. It had begun with a stalker from the UK who had taken an interest in Maddi's past; she had insisted they travel to London to investigate. *Mistake number one,* he thought, as he leaned back in his seat. They had then gone to the Queen's Ball, where not only did someone kill the U.S. Secretary of State, but someone tried to kill Maddi with a dose of poison. That was when Seacroft had become acquainted with Matt Henderson. At first, he had suspected Matt of being involved in the murder attempt, but, after the man subsequently saved her life, it was clear that he hadn't been trying to hurt her, but to keep her safe. Once she recovered, she insisted they go to Latvia to research Eastern Europe's contributions to NATO, "*...in case I elect to go to the conference.*" That had been mistake number two. It had seemed innocent enough, until she ditched him and Brooks at the Riga train station and took off with a stranger – or so he had thought – and traveled west to Latvia's coast. They had managed to find her at a hidden compound by the Baltic Sea, and Seacroft soon learned that the property belonged to the Hendersons. He and Brooks had scaled the gate – which was when Brooks sprained his ankle – and it was then they decided that the bunker-like protections of the estate would be the senator's safest refuge. But then, yesterday morning, she had insisted that they leave that sanctuary at once and fly to Paris, so Maddi could help Matt and Hank save Roger. Soon after they arrived, Maddi received a text from Matt saying that he and Hank were trapped in a cave with the dying Roger and they needed help. So, of course, they had to try to save them. *Mistake number three.* They managed to get to Roger in time, but, in the meantime, Matt was taken by Cobra, which is how the three of them were now on a high-speed train heading southeast to Lyon. *No wonder I'm tired.*

He looked across the aisle at Brooks. The agent was resting peacefully, his head against the side of the train, his sprained ankle propped on his travel bag. *At least someone's getting sleep.* He looked again at Maddi. Her hair fell across her face as she, too, tried to sleep. But her expression was not nearly so peaceful. Her brow was creased and her eyes fluttered beneath the lids. Her face had grown thin from the stress of the past two weeks, and Seacroft was suddenly overcome by the need to keep her safe. She was a remarkable woman who had been through too much. The desire to hug her was overwhelming...and totally inappropriate. He looked away and checked his watch. *An hour to go.* A friend of his in Lyon, a fellow agent, Ethan Bouton, had agreed to meet them at the train. Seacroft had called him the minute he knew they were going to Lyon. Bouton had offered to check out Place Bellecour, including the Hotel le Royal, and make it safe for their arrival. Though Seacroft trusted the man, he wished he had been able to go on ahead and prepare things himself. Those who were trying to kill the senator were not only devious, but clever, too; he had learned to never underestimate them.

But Bouton was a good agent. He had spent nearly eleven months in America during the Clinton years serving with the French Embassy's Security staff, and he and Seacroft had become friends. They had gone through a lot together, including the scandals that had plagued that administration. They had learned rather quickly that they could rely on one another for discretion; a must during the Clinton presidency.

He closed his eyes and tried to sleep. After five minutes, he gave up and looked out at the scenery. They were traveling on a *Train a Grande Vitesse* – TGV – a high-speed supersonic, and there was little to enjoy in the way of landscape. It raced by like a reel of film in fast-forward, and he soon lost himself to his worries once again. He looked at Maddi. Her eyes were no longer fluttering. He grinned; she had finally fallen asleep. He reached over and pulled the jacket she was wearing – Matt Henderson's jacket – tighter to her chin. He hadn't seen that sort of peace on her face for weeks, and, again, he choked back the urge to hug her. *Stop it, Seacroft.*

"Now you can't get too close to 'em, agent." The laconic growl of Sam Allen was comforting, and Seacroft nodded as the man continued. "Guard 'em, protect 'em, even like 'em if you must; but don't ever get too close."

Seacroft had had difficulty with that edict, though he understood it. Like a mother protecting a child, he would become useless if he allowed his emotions to interfere. But no one was more ferocious – or more effective – than a mother bear protecting her cub.

He was aware of the connection between his overarching desire to care for his protectees and the murder of his parents when he was only fourteen years old. The agency shrink had suggested that he would be tempted to substitute the protectees for his mother and father, and that he needed to be careful not to do so, as the emotional attachment would render him ineffective. But he had ignored the recommendation and felt he had done a better job because of it. Though there had been several attempts on the lives of those he had looked after, he had managed to stop every attack, even taking a bullet in the shoulder for a vice-presidential candidate he had covered in 1999.

He had been criticized for that incident, however. His relationship with the candidate – a female – was close; some thought too close, and those above him felt he had let her control the agenda. "She manipulated you...it got you both in trouble."

He had argued the point, insisting his job was not to dictate the protectee's actions; only to keep her safe, regardless of where she was or who she was with. "They can't live in a bubble, now, can they?" He was probably the only agent to receive both a commendation and a reprimand for the same incident.

When he was later asked to justify not only that incident, but his entire method of protecting those he served, he had said calmly; "I care about those I protect. It's that simple." That reply had gotten him a stiff rebuke, but Director Allen had defended him to the higher-ups. Seacroft's record was flawless, and those who might question his approach were compelled to acknowledge that fact. But Allen was instructed to keep his eye on the young agent.

From then on, the director had done his best to avoid placing Seacroft with anyone who might try to control the agenda. And, in turn, Seacroft had done his best to rein in any personal feelings he might have toward those he was asked to look after. Feelings and attachments had a way of backfiring; he knew he had to be careful. "Check your emotions at the door, Seacroft...."

He sighed as he looked at the senator sleeping next to him. *We've gone through a lot together...it's binding.* His fondness for her was matched only by his need to keep her safe. *I'm simply being conscientious...doing my job for a well-respected member of the United States Senate.*

He looked outside and watched the landscape come alive as the train slowed around a curve. The countryside in France looked a lot like home; green hills, farmland, and trees in every direction. Other than the occasional row of grapes, he might have been in Indiana or Illinois; not the southern reaches of France on a daredevil mission to save a Henderson from certain death.

He looked at Maddi. As he watched her sleep, he knew exactly who she was dreaming about; exactly who she was longing to see. He had witnessed the unspoken goodbye between the two of them back at the estate in Latvia; it was the strongest expression of love he had ever seen. *And they hadn't said a word.* He shook his head, knowing there was no other course for Maddi and her agents; the protection of the senator was completely centered around finding – and saving – Matt Henderson. The risks notwithstanding, Seacroft was certain that if they didn't get to him in time, Maddi's life would be over regardless.

Chapter 4

Washington, DC

Edward Morningstar, top aide to the Pentagon's Chairman of the Joint Chiefs, woke up in a sweat. He stared at the ceiling of the hotel suite bedroom, and ran a hand through his clipped black hair. He had been dreaming. And in that dream, he had been piloting a revolutionary warship...a plane, of sorts, which was, ironically, referred to as the Morning Star. Though he had never actually seen the aircraft, he knew it was real; Simeon had confirmed it. And Morningstar was eager to get his hands on it.

He had received little more than a two-minute phone call from his soldier-son, Simeon, about four hours ago regarding the status of the vessel. Simeon had used a payphone to call him, his phone apparently seized by the group he had just become affiliated with, the Morning Star. The name was a reference to a Nazi-era warship they had been assigned to protect. According to Simeon, the group had taken his phone as a precaution. Not only had he been forced to use a payphone, but he had had to speak cryptically, and, as a result, Morningstar knew little of the fate of his ship.

And it truly was *his* warship. He had uncovered evidence just hours ago that basically proved that the Morning Star warship had been named after his grandfather, Heinrich Morningstar, who had apparently been an exceptional Nazi fighter pilot.

Had it made Edward uneasy to learn that his grandfather was a Nazi? Perhaps, but that uneasiness had been short-lived once he realized that the man had been so adept in the cockpit of a plane that Hitler had dedicated a state-of-the-art warship to him. Which meant, by rights, that ship belonged to Morningstar.

The fact that Simeon could tell him anything about the vessel had come about as a result of Simeon's success at playing the role of Johnny Canterbury, the lost heir to a founding member of the elite Morning Star organization. The highbrows had let Simeon in as a provisional member. Which meant that Morningstar now had eyes and ears within one of the most prestigious – and secret – organizations ever established.

Simeon had told him earlier that evening that the group suspected that Dolf Mueller, Germany's vice-chancellor, had stolen a truck carrying the vessel, and had driven it into a vast stretch of mountains that lay between Montbard, France, and Germany's western border. In response, Morningstar had sent another one of his sons, Naphtali, to France to kill Mueller and take the warship. Had he succeeded?

According to Simeon, he had...at least with the first half of the task. Mueller had been killed in an air attack – likely by Naphtali – and his army had been taken out by the Morning Star's private army. But those soldiers had been killed, as well, which meant that, should Naphtali find the warship, Morningstar would have little trouble claiming it as his own. He would have to contend with the elites of the organization, but that shouldn't be too difficult. Other than their leader, a man they referred to as the Caretaker, only Walter Henderson possessed true military experience. The rest were just blustering old fools caught up in their own self-importance. And, from what Simeon had told him, they were so undone by the Caretaker's death, they were pretty much useless.

Simeon's call had come soon after the members had left their all-night meeting, around eight a.m. in Paris, which was two a.m. in America. They had been instructed to go back to their rooms and get some rest. That was when Simeon had snuck out of the hotel and had walked the four blocks to a payphone. Morningstar had insisted that he forego his nap and look for the vessel. *"Find Naphtali. Then the two of you need to search every crag until you find the damn warship, Simeon."*

Simeon had replied, *"It won't be that simple, Father. For one thing, we're all supposed to meet again at one o'clock. There isn't enough time for me to find Naphtali, let alone the vessel, and get back in time for the meeting. For another thing, even if I find Naphtali, it won't be just he and I who are searching those mountains."* Simeon had gone on to say that Walter had brought in a team of soldiers from his private Latvian army to scour the mountains for the missing vessel. This was after he had already pulled in three of his men to protect the warehouse where the ship had originally been hidden. Morningstar had bristled. *"I'm so damn tired of a Henderson always getting in my way!"* They had left it that Simeon would use the time before the one o'clock meeting to find Naphtali. The two could then work together to hunt for the vessel once the meeting was over.

But Morningstar's fresh anger with the Hendersons had given him an idea. With Walter in Paris, and so many of his Latvian soldiers there, as well, his compound – the stately Henderson castle – would be far less protected than usual. Morningstar grinned. *It's time for me to send Walter and his clan a message.*

He slid out of bed, not wanting to wake the woman next to him, his lovely paramour, Janet. Not because he was thoughtful; the bitch was there for him, not the other way around. No, it was out of a need to have at least a few minutes to himself. He didn't have time for her tempting sensuality...not now; there was too much going on. He had to have his mind clear and his body focused for what he was about to do.

He grabbed his cellphone from a table by the bed and crept into the bathroom. He closed the door and dialed a preprogrammed number. When it was answered, he whispered, "Zebulun, it is time. I'll send instructions to the website." He ended the call, not waiting for a reply. His Russian soldier-son would take it from there.

He set the phone by the sink, relieved himself, then brushed his teeth. Today was turning out to be even more eventful than expected. While Zebulun was delivering a message to the Hendersons in Latvia, Morningstar would be delivering his own message to some bigwigs in DC. And it would start with the weekly meeting of the Bentley Group, the secret organization that had padded the pockets of a select assortment of Beltway players for the past six years. Morningstar had joined the group three years ago, and had transformed them from a gathering of greedy old men, to his very own launching pad for changing the world order.

Today's meeting would get him one step closer.

He took a quick shower, then walked out to the living room in nothing but a towel. He went to the window and looked outside, noticing the hint of yellow that had begun to creep over the DC skyline. *Awaken the world, sun.* He chuckled as a sudden ray of sunlight lit up the Capitol dome...bowing to his directive. It was fitting. Every major event seemed to offer him a new opportunity to advance his plan. And this morning, he was about to deliver a bombshell.

Time to get on with it, he thought, as he walked back to the bathroom and dried his hair. He went to the hotel suite's closet, picked out his finest suit among the three he had brought from home, and put it on. He admired himself as he stood in front of a gilded full-length mirror, chuckling as he put on cufflinks and smoothed his lapels. *You are truly dashing, Morningstar.*

He walked again to the living room, went to a desk, and opened his laptop. After four passcodes on four different sites, he reached the website where he linked with his sons. In cryptic sentences, with the help of maps and overhead surveillance video, he outlined his mission for his Russian soldier, Zebulun. He logged off and slid the laptop into his briefcase, along with his government-issued sat phone. He put the other phone – the cellphone he used to speak with the sons of Jacob – in his pocket.

Now, on to the Bentley Group. From his desk, he grabbed two documents he had typed the night before. He read them through and nodded. As he folded each one and tucked them into his suit coat pocket, he grinned. Late last night, his boss, five-star General Alexander Daniels, had received a 'leaked document' from an unnamed source, and had, of course, promptly called Morningstar. The document implied that the Vice-president, Jim Conner was involved in '...*questionable arms deals,*' and was about to be indicted. The revelation would be earth-shattering to an administration that, up to then, had been one of the more respected in the nation's history. President James Wilcox had shown himself to be a man of integrity. He had gone out of his way to be nonpartisan, and his word was gold among members of Congress. It was a rare attribute, and, as a result, he enjoyed high approval ratings from both the country and the world. The indictment of one of his closest allies – his *Vice-president,* no less – would destroy the trust he had garnered over the last four years. And, in an election year, the other side would feast on the news like maggots on a carcass. *"Shut it down, Morningstar,"* Daniels had told him. *"I'll handle it, sir,"* he had dutifully replied.

He put on his overcoat, picked up his briefcase, and, without a word to his slumbering concubine, he walked out the door. The air was cool and he buttoned his coat as he walked to the corner to wave down a cab. Normally, he had a driver pick him up, but he had made it clear that on Mondays no driver was needed. It was vital that he keep his affiliation with the Bentley Group a secret. It was vital that *all* of them keep their affiliation a secret. It was that fact that would allow him to pull off this morning's plan.

A cab pulled to the curb and he slid in back. "The Morgan Building," he said as he leaned back in the seat. He tried to imagine the country's surprise should it learn that Vice-president James Conner was a member of a secret group whose sole purpose was to advance war for the sake of profit. Justifying it as an "America first," policy, the men in that organization were actually padding their own pockets. Every one of them had a hand in the arms production apparatus, and every time they instigated a war, or even the threat of one, their profits skyrocketed.

Morningstar had been asked to join the group three years ago, by the Vice-president himself. And, as he tended to do with whatever he was involved in, he had elevated the organization. No longer did those old men just wait for wars to occur. Now, with his clever guidance, they pushed the buttons and pulled the levers to make war happen. Though to a man they pretended to find it unconscionable, every one of them accepted their hefty payouts without complaint.

The cab turned onto Morgan Street and stopped in front of a tall, nondescript building. Morningstar paid the driver, then got out and ran up the steps to the Morgan Building. For six years, the group had met there every Monday before the work day began. On most of those mornings, the meetings were boring and predictable. But on this particular Monday, those men were in for a big surprise. Not one of them

28

would ever know that it was Morningstar who had orchestrated all that was about to happen. They had no idea what he was capable of. They all assumed it was the vice-president who controlled the agenda. He laughed. *They're about to see what I can do.*

He walked into the lobby and made his way to the elevators, grinning at his own cleverness. It was he who had written the unsigned memo that had caused such a stir with Daniels. The 'leak' he had so carefully arranged suggested irregularities with arms trades between Silverton Industries and the U.S. Army. Those trades, according to the anonymous memo, had been proffered solely by one man...the vice-president of the United States, James Conner. With exquisite detail, Morningstar had created memos and altered files to make it look as if Conner had acted alone. Daniels had been stunned when he had seen the evidence. *"The country will not be well-served by such a scandal,"* he had told Morningstar. *"Do your best to keep it out of the news."*

So, Morningstar had put together a solution; a way out for Conner, and a way for the Wilcox Administration to save face. And all the while, the entire exercise would put Morningstar one step closer to his goal. He patted the documents inside his suit coat and chuckled. *Here I come, Bentley Group, to move us all to the next level.*

He waited for the elevator door to open, then stepped inside with three other men. He slid to the back. When the last man had left the elevator, he inserted a key in a slot to the side, then waited as he was taken to the top floor. The doors opened to the familiar meeting room where he and the others had fueled revolutions and ignited wars with little more than a flourish of a cigar. Two Secret-Service agents were standing by the door, out of earshot of the proceedings, but close enough to watch over their protectee, the U.S. vice-president. Morningstar, who had initially challenged their presence, had been reassured that they had been paid handsomely to 'look the other way.' He had felt some relief when he learned that one of the men was married to Conner's niece. *Family doesn't sell out family...usually.* Nonetheless, he would have preferred that they weren't there. Being able to identify the members of that group was a risk for every man in the room. But he had been overruled. *"The government gave me that protection for a reason, Morningstar...I'm important."*

Whatever, Morningstar thought as he walked past the two agents into the room. He was almost to his seat when he stopped. He walked back and motioned for the taller agent to bend down so he could whisper in his ear. "Don't forget, Johnson, I know about your trips to the Caymans." The agent's eyes widened and he tugged at his collar, his face as white as a sheet. Morningstar grinned as he straightened his tie and walked to his chair. *That should shut him up.*

There were no windows in the room, and the only entrance was the elevator. Masterpieces hung on each wall. A chandelier was centered over a solid oak table, circled by eight plush chairs. The room was posh, private, and perfect for their needs.

Morningstar dropped his briefcase by his chair, then took off his overcoat and carried it to a closet. He hung it up, then walked to a sideboard where he poured a cup of coffee. He sipped it as he sauntered slowly to his seat.

"Hurry up, Morningstar. You're late."

It was Conner, and Morningstar had to fight not to laugh. *In a matter of minutes, you'll no longer be such a pain in my ass.* "Yes, I know. I apologize. I have some big news, however."

He always had big news; he *was* the news. Without him, nothing would happen; they would be little more than a group of stodgy old men trying to eek a bit of profit from arms sales in DC. *I have made this group what it is.*

He took another sip of coffee, then pulled out a cigar. He clipped it just below the cap line and lit it slowly, taking several puffs to allow the aroma to fill his lungs.

"Holy shit, Morningstar...get on with it!"

Conner again.

Morningstar tightened his jaw. "I have some bad news...and I have some good news. Which do you want first?"

"Geez, Morningstar...quit playing games."

"Which do you want first?"

"Fine. Give us the bad news."

Morningstar forced a melancholy sigh. "Well, sir, I'm sorry to report that you – the Vice-President – are about to be indicted by Congress for illegal arms trading."

Conner's face grew white and his hands trembled as he set his coffee on the table. "What the hell are you talking about, Morningstar?"

Morningstar held his expression. "A communique was leaked to someone at the Pentagon, who then leaked it to my boss. I'm not yet sure who's behind the leak, but once I find out, you can rest assured, sir, I will make his life a living hell."

Conner pushed back from the table, his large frame unsteady as he stood and paced back and forth. "This...this is crazy, Morningstar!" He stopped and looked at the men at the table. "Aren't any of the rest of you involved in this *indictment?*"

Morningstar shook his head. "No, thank God. And we're fortunate you're the man you are and won't pull any of us into this investigation." Morningstar took another sip of coffee, looking over the rim at the others. Their faces had also grown white, his last comment doing little to quell their concerns. He set his cup on the table, took another drag on his cigar, and pulled the two folded documents from inside his suit coat. "Are you ready for the good news?"

Conner ran his thick hands through his wild gray hair. He leaned on his chair, gripping it as if he was clinging to a life raft. "Yeah, and it better be *real* good."

"Because of my role at the Pentagon, and the popularity of your boss, Wilcox, I've been able to pull some strings. I've put together an arrangement, of sorts." He unfolded one of the documents. "What I have here, Chief, is your agreement to resign from the administration, effective immediately, citing problems at home."

Conner's face was now bright red, his cheeks puffed out in fury. "But I don't have any problems at home!"

"You do now, sir." Morningstar cleared his throat, fighting a grin. "Your wife of forty years has threatened to leave you."

Conner swept his coffee cup off the table. It hit the carpeted floor, splashing black coffee all over the plush white rug. "What the hell are you talking about, Morningstar? Betsy wouldn't leave me...hell, the woman worships me!"

"Not any more. She's been told of your...activities...and insists on a divorce."

Conner's legs were shaking and he continued to cling to the back of his chair. The blood drained from his face as he spun the chair around and slumped onto the seat. He put his head in his hands. "Dear god, my life is ruined."

"Not exactly, sir. If you resign today, Betsy has agreed to stay with you. She doesn't want the humiliation of a congressional hearing, and with your resignation, the charges disappear. Then you can get to work on fixing your troubled marriage."

The room was silent. Of all the bombshells that had been dropped in that chamber, none compared to what Morningstar had just said. The men were hushed. He knew they were worried, not for Conner, but for themselves.

Conner kept shaking his head and mumbling. After a minute, he looked up with bloodshot eyes. "Why do I get the feeling that you're more involved in this than you say, Morningstar?"

"Trust me, sir; this isn't good for me, either. It's your stewardship that has led us to where we are today. I just feel fortunate to be able to intercede on your behalf." Morningstar swallowed, the words nearly choking him. He took a quick puff on his cigar. "Daniels knows it's in the country's best interest that no one ever get wind of this. The only thing you have to do, sir, is never breathe a word of your involvement with this group or with any of us at this table, other than what might be expected through normal government channels."

Morningstar allowed the words to sink in while he took another drag on his cigar. He blew the smoke in rings, watching as they floated like clouds to the ceiling.

Senator Franks from Nebraska said, "What about the rest of us? Are we safe from this investigation?"

"Yes, as long as Conner keeps his mouth shut."

All eyes turned to Conner. He raised his head; his face was once again ruddy red. "You're an asshole, Morningstar! I know that you are somehow behind this!"

Morningstar cleared his throat. "As I said, Conner, I, too, am losing in this situation...we all are. Your guidance will be missed."

Conner glared at him, then looked around the room, weighing the expressions of each of the men, not one of them willing to look him in the eye. "Let me get this straight, Morningstar. If I go quietly into the night, resign from the ticket of my Commander in Chief, go home to my wife Betsy and make 'amends'...you have ensured that nothing will happen to me. Is that what you're telling me?"

"Yes, that's about it, sir."

"How can you do that? How can you make an arms violation just disappear?"

It was Morningstar's turn to bristle. He slammed his fist on the table, causing coffee to splatter. "Dammit! It's what I've been trying to tell you all along. I'm the powerful one here. I'm the one with connections. It is I who know the right people and can pull the right strings." His hands were shaking, and he forced a drag on his cigar. Quieter, he said, "Maybe now, you will all appreciate what I'm capable of."

No one said a word. A clock on the wall ticked off the seconds as the men stared at the table. Finally, Conner said, "What if I give you all up?" It was the unspoken fear that haunted each of them. Not one raised his head to look at their former 'chief.' Conner glared at Morningstar. "What's the worst that could happen?"

Morningstar said coolly, "Oh, I don't know. Tried for treason by your country...imprisoned for life...left by your adoring wife. What's better: the justification you might feel by taking us all down with you, or a peaceful retirement with your dear wife in your spacious compound on Nantucket?" He leaned forward, practically blowing smoke in the VP's face. "Which *we* and *our efforts* helped you purchase, don't forget." He sat back. "You tell me which option is best."

Conner wiped his forehead. Though the room was cool, he was sweating, and Morningstar thought the man might have a stroke. *Not here, dammit...wait until you've left the building, at least.* He could see the strain – the agony – on the man's face. Conner had been with Wilcox for nearly ten years; first as his Chief of Staff in the Pennsylvania Governor's mansion, then as his running mate four years ago. It was killing Conner, and Morningstar almost felt sorry for him. The VP said evenly, "Does Wilcox know anything about this?"

"Not yet. As I say, Daniels has given me wide berth on this. I think you all need to grasp the risk I've taken to make this go away. I have convinced Daniels that it would be best if *no one* knows of it; not even the President. It's an election year; a good time to make a change in running mates. You've got a good excuse, Conner. The timing is perfect for your exit...and I suggest you take it."

"Who will replace me?"

Morningstar took another drag on his cigar, knowing every man in the room was hanging on his reply. "There's a senator from Florida...a swing state, as you know. The President has been in touch with him in preparation for several visits he plans to make as the election gets closer. The guy would be perfect. As a member of Congress, he's been well-vetted. And, his respect in Florida has been heralded on many occasions; he's become the darling of the party. He would practically deliver Florida to the win column for Wilcox." He added. "Not that he'll need it, of course."

Conner shook his head. Though his face was a red ball of anger, his eyes showed something different; they showed grief. Conner hadn't always played by the rules, but he loved DC; the parades, the pageantry, the power. And now, suddenly, it was over. *The bigger they are...*

Conner pulled the documents in front of him and read them through. The first was his resignation, suggesting a need to return home '...*to spend time with my wife in our house on the Bay.*' The second outlined his sins; arms trading, his involvement – alone – in the exchanges, and his attempt to cover his tracks by using a liaison at Silverton Industries. His temples were pulsing as he took in each line; every sentence either an admission or a concession. "I can't sign either of these pieces of bullshit!"

Morningstar said calmly, "You have no other choice." He paused. "Why don't you take a minute to think it over. Maybe even give Betsy a call...get her take on the matter." He stifled a grin. "We'll wait here."

Conner glared over his glasses at Morningstar. Morningstar stared back with cold, dark eyes; his expression a blank wall of indifference. He didn't give a damn about Conner, and Conner knew it. And Morningstar wasn't worried about the call to Betsy; he had already shored up her participation. *Amazing where our secrets will lead us.* A simple reminder of a sordid affair she had had years ago, and – voilà – she was eager to support her husband, as long as he left the Vice-Presidency behind. "Go ahead, Conner...you can use the back room. We'll wait here, right boys?"

The other men stared back and forth between Morningstar and Conner. A few of them nodded weakly. Morningstar knew what they were thinking. *"There but for the grace of Morningstar, go I."*

Conner stood and stumbled out of the room. As he left, Morningstar looked at the others and grinned. "So, boys, how about those Dodgers?"

Conner's legs felt unsteady as he walked to a back room. *That son-of-a-bitch!* Despite Morningstar's claims to the contrary, Conner was certain the Pentagon aide was behind it. The prick had been looking for a way to undermine him since he had joined the Bentley Group. Conner found a wingback chair which faced an original Picasso, *The Weeping Woman.* He sat and stared at the painting, shaking as he pulled out his phone. Should he call Betsy? How could he? Through forty years of marriage, he had never disappointed her. At least not in the ways that mattered. He had had an affair or two, but she had never known. Besides, those women hadn't meant a thing to him. Just hollow flings to offset the tedium of DC. He sighed and stared at his phone. Finally, with a shaking hand, he dialed.

A quiet voice said, "Hello?"

"Betsy, it's me. Are you aware...of the bullshit going on?"

Silence. Then, "Jimmy, it's time to hang it up."

Dear god...this is really happening. "Betsy, it's not true."

More silence. "Does it matter?"

Conner frowned. *Does it matter? Hell yes, it matters! This is horseshit!* But he knew what she meant...and she was right. Regardless of the merit of the claim — and there was plenty of that — he was caught. In whatever web had been strung together by those who wanted him out of the way, he was caught. "But Betsy, I—"

"Just sign the papers, Jimmy."

He stared at the Picasso. He was having trouble catching his breath. He didn't know how or why the pieces had fallen together as they had, but he knew one thing; sooner or later he would learn who was behind it. For whatever reason, he was being forced from his role as VP, and Betsy was somehow on board. *Who has the power — or the connections — to make such a thing happen?* He knew the answer: Morningstar. And, though he had clearly underestimated the man's clout at the Pentagon, he had known all along that he was devious. *Hell...I benefited from it...more than once.*

He sighed. "Okay, baby. I'll sign them." He paused. "But you'll still be there for me, right? Waiting for me on the veranda at the house in Nantucket?"

There was a pause. "Sure baby. Come on home."

Conner said nothing and ended the call. He slid his phone in his pocket and stood, still staring at the Picasso. The painting was unsettling; misshapen body parts attached in all the wrong places. *How fitting,* he thought as he finally turned and stumbled back to the main room. He had made his decision. Yes, he would sign the papers. *But mark my words, Morningstar, you have not heard the last of me.*

Conner walked into the room, and all eyes turned away...except for Morningstar, who gave him a pointed stare, his gray eyes almost black in the dark room. Conner's eye twitched; he had been about to say something, but must have thought better of it. He walked to his chair and stood behind it, gripping the back as he stared down at the two documents. Without sitting down, he leaned over, pulled a pen from his pocket and scratched his name across the bottom of each. He tossed the pen on the table.

Morningstar grinned. With a simple signature on the bottom of two pieces of paper, Conner had signed away his place in history; his legacy. It was gone. In less than fifteen minutes his world had changed forever.

Morningstar reached for the documents, snapped a picture of the second one with his phone, then folded the documents and returned them to his pocket. He sent the photo to a number that wasn't in his contact list, waited ten seconds, then deleted the photo and the text. He slid the phone in his pocket, then sat back and nodded. "The Silverton representative, your liaison, isn't a well man. He'll soon suffer a heart attack and die. That will end the only witness to suggest that this isn't exactly as these documents say...other than the men in this room." He glanced at those around the table, then looked over his shoulder at the secret service agents. "No one here would dare reveal a thing...they all have too much to lose." He paused to let it sink in as he took another drag on his cigar. "The second document you signed is the insurance policy. It will remain under lock and key, only to be revealed if you give up our secrets. I'll give keys to multiple individuals, just in case there's an idea that eliminating me will eliminate the document." He cleared his throat. "I just sent a photo of the document to a good friend of mine. He's to print out a copy and take it to the nearest newspaper should something happen to me before I can get the documents where they need to go." He took a sip of coffee, then sat back and crossed his legs. "Now, I would be glad to help you arrange for a press conference if you'd like."

Conner glared at him, his eyes on fire. He was gripping his chair and Morningstar knew he was fighting the urge to pick it up and throw it at him. "I don't need your *help,* Morningstar. I can arrange my own damned press conference!"

Morningstar nodded but said nothing as he took another puff on his cigar.

Conner continued to stand with his hands on the chair, his head bowed as the clock on the wall marked the passage of time. No one said a word, their silence perhaps a show of respect, or, more likely, an echo of fear for their own fates.

After several minutes, Conner stepped back from his chair. He looked at each of them, his eyes narrowed, his jaw tight. Without a word, he turned and walked to the elevator. His head was bowed and he said nothing as he stepped inside, his two agents following him and standing on each side of him. The door closed; the room was silent. One by one, the other members stood and walked to the elevator. Morningstar stayed where he was, puffing his cigar.

The men stepped into the elevator two at a time, and proceeded down to the lobby. When the last of them was about to get in, he looked at Morningstar and said, "How can you be so sure that Wilcox will pick the Florida senator?"

Morningstar grinned. "Don't worry...he'll pick him. Trust me on that one."

The man narrowed his eyes. "Which one is it...which senator?"

Morningstar blew smoke in the air. "His name is Knight...Jerome Knight."

39

CHAPTER 5

Ikla, Estonia

"Zebulun will live by the seashore and become a haven for ships." The declaration from Genesis 49:13 rang through Vladimir Karev's head like a broken record. But, unlike the repetitive refrain from an annoying song, the words were uplifting, and he smiled as he wiped dirt from his hands and walked from the docks in the small town of Ikla, Estonia. Though it was only midday, his work had come to an end. A simple phone call had changed everything.

The sun was high in the sky, and he stopped to look at it one last time. It lit up the sea like a midnight raid from Putin's air force. He never tired of it; the bold yellow rays shimmering on the unbridled waves of the Baltic. He breathed in, mist filling his lungs, reviving him as he greeted the restful reprieve of the sea. He had never known such beauty, such peace, until he moved to the coast, and he was angry as he imagined the other sights and smells he had missed through his twenty-six years of life. *Never again will I pledge my allegiance to fools.*

Moving to the Estonia city had been Jacob's idea. And, like every other recommendation from the American, it had been a good one. Though it was bitterly cold most of the year, it was far more uplifting than his native Siberia. The people were kinder; as if their struggles were merely against the cold...*instead of misery and despair.* It was in Estonia he had waited, spending his days toiling as a longshoreman on the Baltic coast. Why? *Because Jacob has asked it of me.*

Men like Jacob – Edward Morningstar – were rare, and Vladimir had seen it immediately: his dignity, his discipline, his lack of emotion. He expected obedience, and Vladimir was eager to comply. Jacob's presence in his life had changed him in a way he had not imagined; for the first time in as long as he could remember, he had sensed a future filled with purpose. Jacob had promised him that if he joined his family and became one of his sons, then, together, they would conquer the world.

That had been nearly four years ago, and, in that time, Vladimir had readied himself for the task. Not just physically, but mentally. *"I'll need you to be the fastest and the strongest, my son, but – most importantly – I'll need you to be the smartest."* Jacob had added, *"You must learn about America…the geography, the customs, the way the people look, the things that make them laugh."* Vladimir had done it; he had made himself tougher and harder…and he had learned about America. It was likely he felt the pulse of that country better than many of the privileged who grew up there.

When he wasn't studying, he worked on the docks…day in, day out, unloading barges, then stacking them again. He kept to himself, knowing that to make a friend was to potentially foster an enemy. *Something I learned in Russia.* He had let his coal black hair grow past his shoulders, along with a heavy beard and mustache. He kept a low profile, formed no alliances, forged no friendships as he waited to hear from Jacob. And, as he waited, he learned…about the United States of America. Its history, its form of government, the attack on New York's World Trade Center in 2001 and the wars that followed, and the resistance to those wars as Americans tired of sacrificing for a country that they cared nothing about. He was stunned such resistance would be tolerated. He learned about the Miami Marlins baseball team that had won the World Series the year before, about Madonna, Brittney, and Lord of the Rings. But mostly, he learned about himself; that he was resilient and strong…that he could fit in anywhere, yet stay hidden...that he was, in fact, a chameleon.

He was eager to see her...this America, so overindulged, yet so full of hope. Vladimir had known little hope in his life. His mother was cruel, his father weak, his country wicked. But America seemed filled with optimism...as seen in their courage during World War II, or their certainty in the race to the moon. But the best example was evident in their willingness – their sheer moxie – to go up against Britain's King George III in April of 1775. Reading about those brave and determined soldiers of the Revolutionary War had made him want to declare his own independence...from his home, from Russia, from its corrupt leaders. And, by joining Morningstar's team, that was exactly what he was doing. *I will go to America...and feel the power of freedom.*

But he had become impatient. Days had turned into weeks had turned into months, and he had grown tired of waiting. Each day it had become harder; each night had made him wonder if – just maybe – it had all been a hoax. He had started to question whether Morningstar as Jacob with his twelve soldier-sons was even real.

Which was why the call he had received just minutes ago had been so welcome. *"Zebulun, it is time."* Those four words had suddenly made all of it real.

He smiled as he turned away from the sea and walked the half-mile to his home. He climbed the stairs to his small apartment, eager to get on his laptop and learn what Jacob had planned for him. He guessed it involved America; why else would Jacob have asked that he learn so much about the country?

He opened the door, walked in, and quickly locked the door behind him. He threw his pack on the table and pulled out his laptop, the only piece of technology he owned, other than his phone. He logged into a secure website, pulled up an article about 1922 Russia, then waited. Within minutes, a link appeared within the article. He clicked it and it took him to another link, which he also clicked. He was taken to a password-protected page. He typed in the password he had been given four years ago, and was pleased when he saw a page of emails pop up on his screen. He opened the most recent and began poring through the attachments. He was disappointed to see that the mission didn't involve America. *Why did I do all that studying?* he wondered as he pored through maps and diagrams not of America, but of Latvia, less than a day away by train. Irritated, he wrote out a text to Jacob, his hands shaking as he waited to push send. Would it anger him? Would he be disappointed in Zebulun for questioning his plan? He looked out the only window at the revealing sunlight and sighed. *I did not spend all this time here and do all this studying simply to have my task change on a whim.* He pushed send, then sat back and rubbed his eyes. The response came within seconds. *"Consider this a practice run,"* was all it said. Zebulun took a deep breath, holding it as he pondered the reply. Finally, he nodded. It was the right answer. How could he expect to carry out a vital task in America without rehearsing it first?

With renewed vigor, he spent the next half-hour reviewing his mission. There was a well-protected compound on Latvia's west coast that he was to infiltrate, and, once there, a man he was to kill. The man's photo had been included. There was also a memo he was to put in an envelope, which he would leave by the dead man's body. When he had read through the mission in its entirety, he sent another text. *"What is the goal, Father?"* Jacob's reply: *"To send a message, son...and to start a war."*

He logged off the laptop and slid it into his backpack. He was ready. He walked to the bathroom, peeled off his clothes, and stepped under the shower. He turned it as hot as it would go. After a few minutes, when his skin was as red as the Soviet flag, he stepped out, dried quickly, and stared at the mirror. He wiped away the steam and stared at his face. His forehead was broad and weathered, his right cheek marked by a scar from a run-in with a caribou, and his eyes were ice-blue, like the Kara Sea in winter. His beard nearly covered his lips and cheeks, and his black, wet hair hung in strands past his shoulders. He tied it back with a rubber band and nodded. *You are ready, Vladimir Karev.*

He put on dark jeans and a black sweatshirt. He stuffed his few belongings in his backpack, including a pair of night goggles. He yanked up two floorboards and pulled out three M-18 smoke grenades, a shoulder-fired missile, and a well-oiled AK47, which he took apart and laid carefully on top. He zipped the backpack, then took two Ka-bar knives from the opening in the floor and slid them in a pocket of his jacket. Though he was good with a rifle, he was even better with a knife.

He replaced the floorboards, then scrubbed the walls, the woodwork, the appliances. He had to remove any evidence that could link him to Ikla. His DNA might soon be important and he needed his name, along with his history, to remain unknown. He walked into the bathroom and did the same, picking up stray hairs by the shower drain, scrubbing toothpaste from around the faucet. *I will leave here as I have lived...unnoticed.*

He took a final look around. Afternoon shadows had begun to fill the room as he said goodbye to the tenement where he had lived for nearly four years...the tenement where he had learned what it meant to be a man...the tenement where he had finally discovered his purpose in life. He pulled on a parka over his jacket and situated a black beret – his father's – on top of his head. With his backpack on his shoulder, he walked out of the apartment, then down the stairs and out the door, squinting as the sunlight assaulted his eyes. He took a look around at the small town that had been his home, his launching pad to the world. He would miss it; the apartment, the village, the Baltic Sea which greeted him every morning like a lover. *Perhaps I will return someday.*

He marched silently to the train station. As he said goodbye to Ikla, he smiled, the depth of his understanding now coursing a river through his soul. Ikla had been his teacher...every bit as much as Morningstar. He took a last look over his shoulder, eying the sun's reflection on the sea, surprised to feel a tear on his cheek. He wiped it away and nodded. *With the strength of the sun and the power of the sea, I, Vladimir Karev, have now become...Zebulun.*

Chapter 6

Baclayon, in the Philippines

Samuels wiped his handkerchief across his sweating forehead as he leaned forward in the taxi. He had given the driver Mark Villamor's home address outside Baclayon and was uneasy as he watched the scenery change from patchy grasslands to even more isolated country. The dirt roads that had taken him to the boarding school were now nothing more than gravel paths, and the overgrown brush along each side felt like it was swallowing him as he sat in the back of the old sedan.

His stomach was once again in fits, a combination of the uneven road and his anxiety as he tried to imagine who – or what – he might find at the Villamor house. Would there be evidence of Mark's upbringing; something to tell him of the pain the poor boy had suffered at the hand of the headmaster? Though he knew it wasn't the Villamor's themselves who had misused the trust of a small boy, he couldn't help but wonder why they had sat by and done nothing as their child was being brutalized at the school. Surely Mark had told them what was happening. How could they have ignored it? Tough questions...with tough answers, he was sure. He was eager to uncover the truth. But it had been over ten years since Mark had lived in Baclayon. It was likely the parents had moved...or maybe even died. *Or were perhaps killed?*

The cab slowed and pulled up to a cottage in the middle of nowhere. He stared through the cab's window, doing his best to take it all in. The house was small – maybe only four or five rooms – and there was an overgrown hedge on each side of what looked like the remnants of a stone walkway. The stones were cracked and weeds had grown up in-between. He sighed as he stared at the forgotten house. *I'll bet it was charming at one time,* he thought, imagining a lovely coastal cottage.

He checked his cellphone to see if the Inspector had tried to call, and was concerned when he saw that he had no service. A shiver ran through him as he looked at the house. *Hopefully, I'll not need to make any phone calls.*

With his travel bag over his shoulder and his jacket folded over one arm, he stepped from the cab, then leaned in and said, "Could you wait again, please?" The cabby sighed, but gave a reluctant nod. Samuels handed him a hundred-peso note.

He turned and followed the walkway to the house. As he got closer, he could hear the sound of waves hitting the coastline just beyond a row of trees that sat behind the modest home. Though it was soothing, it was also unsettling...as if the calming sea was mocking his descent into the maelstrom. He thought of his favorite quote from the Poe narrative, "*...but in the next moment I cursed myself for being so great a fool as to dream of hope at all.*" Was that the case here? Was he foolish to think he could somehow save Cobra's alter ego? He shook his head. *I must try.*

He continued down the walk, rubbing the back of his neck as the late day sun beat down on him. He took a labored breath; he felt as if he was suffocating, not only from the humidity pressing on his chest, but from his anxiety over the meeting he was about to conduct. How should he introduce himself? *"Hello, I'm your son's shrink. He sees me in-between murders."*

He reached the end of the walk and stopped. He looked at the house. It was old and very much alone. *Like me.* The white siding had yellowed, the eaves were dented from years of neglect. He wondered if the home had ever been happy. Had Mark had a joyful childhood before the headmaster had

had his way with him? *Not likely.* Killers like Cobra were rarely crafted from a joyful child. What he was looking at seemed to confirm it. The house was dying, along with everything around it.

Late-day shadows didn't help his anxiety, and he trembled as he climbed two decrepit steps to a narrow front porch. He felt certain that the house had been abandoned, yet he pushed on, needing to see it through. He saw a swing off to the side, barely moving with what little breeze had been summoned through the trees. The swing was old and broken, but Samuels could envision Mark and his mother swinging happily on a summer day while his father was away at work. Had there ever been such a time for the tortured boy?

He walked up to the door and was about to knock when he stopped and put an ear to the door. His eyes widened; he heard the hum of a television. *Someone lives here!* He took a breath, holding it as he knocked firmly on the door. He could hear a shuffling of feet; he gripped his hands into fists to keep them from shaking. The door opened; a woman was standing there. He had to fight not to stare. The bones of her cheeks were far too pronounced; she was nothing but skin and bones. *The poor woman is ill.*

"Can I help you?" she asked, her voice weak, but kind.

Samuels cleared his throat. "Mrs. Villamor?"

"It's 'Miss.' And you are?"

She's still here! He pulled his wallet from his pocket and held up his passport. "I—I'm Dr. James Samuels...a psychiatrist from London. I have recently spent a bit of time with your son. May I come in?"

The woman stared first at the passport, then at him. Her eyes were dark; they looked black in the shadows of late day. She stepped back and motioned him in with a thin, frail hand.

He followed the woman into the house, taking note of the worn carpet and faded woodwork.

"What can I do for you, Dr. Samuels?"

He cleared his throat. "Uh...this past week, I had the occasion of meeting your son, Mark."

Her features tightened. "I see. I'm sorry to hear that."

"No, don't be. I met him under the most unusual circumstances. He has turned out to be a fine young man, you know."

The woman glared at him. "Ha! You mock me! We both know that Mark is not a fine young man, now, don't we?"

Samuels felt as if he had been struck. *What a foolish thing for me to say!*

She went on, the edge to her voice making him uneasy. "Do you know who he is?"

Samuels bowed his head. "Yes ma'am, I do."

She clenched her fists. "Then you know that he is a...very *bad* man."

Softer, he said, "Yes ma'am, I do." He cleared his throat and added quickly, "But there appears to be two sides to him."

She bristled. "'Two sides' describes him well. One dark...the other, darker." She sighed and her features softened. "You've clearly traveled a long way. Can I get you something to drink, Doctor?"

Samuels sighed, relieved. "A glass of water would be welcome, Ma'am."

"You can call me Nenita."

Samuels followed her into a small living room. She walked over and turned off an old Magnavox TV. She motioned to a faded easy chair, then left the room to get his water. He sat and looked around. The room was small, the furnishings outdated and worn. But they weren't cheap. It was clear that at one time, the home had been quite lovely. There was an ornate brown table sitting under a window. It sat next to an Esmerelda sofa that had been washed-out by the sun. There were two chairs; the one he was sitting in, and one where Nenita likely spent most of her time. Though both were of high quality, they had seen better days. He searched for personal items; photos, scrap books, clay sculptures from a child's tender hands...there were none. He was surprised to see a finely-cut crystal bowl sitting on the table; a lavish piece among the less-than-lavish surroundings. Its sharp edges yielded prisms of light that beamed throughout the room; a stark contrast to the muted tones of the walls and curtains. *Waterford crystal?* He continued his inspection, scanning the walls for a family photo or a medal of a child's triumph; there was nothing. The only picture was a masterful reproduction of Rembrandt's, "Old Woman Reading." *Odd,* he thought, *another overstated piece in this understated room.* But the house was clean. There was no dust on the sill; no cobwebs on the ceiling. The works of art notwithstanding, she didn't seem interested in splendor, just in keeping things in order. *Waiting to die.*

So, had the lavish items been gifts, perhaps? Had Mark's father brought them home from travels abroad? He looked again at the painting. He admired Rembrandt. Within every one of his paintings was a strategically-placed glimmer of light intended to contrast hopefulness within a brooding gloom. As he looked at the portrait, he wondered, as so many had before him, *Is she Rembrandt's mother?* The significance of a mother could never be underestimated. *All men reflect the souls of their mothers.* So, what about Cobra? Surely his actions didn't echo the gentle soul of the woman who had been so gracious to welcome Samuels into her home. So how does one explain it? *Perhaps...in the end...we must choose.*

Nenita walked from the kitchen, her faded silk robe hanging loosely on her thin, fragile frame. She was carrying a glass of water in a shaking hand; he felt she might break from the weight of it. She handed it to him, and, as she did, her robe slid back from her wrist. He frowned as he noted a telltale scar. *Somewhere along the way, the poor woman has tried to kill herself.*

She quickly pulled down the sleeve and walked away.

Samuels took a sip of water. "Pardon my boldness, but are you ill?"

The question didn't seem to surprise her. As she shuffled to her chair and fell defeatedly into its reprieve, she looked at him and said softly, "Yes, I have cervical cancer. I was in remission for the longest time, but it has returned, and seems to have won the day." She paused. "A hazard of the profession, I guess."

Samuels frowned. *What profession?* He was about to ask when he thought better of it. "Is your husband home?"

The woman narrowed her eyes. "I don't have a husband. If you're referring to Mark's father, he doesn't live here."

Samuels nodded. "I see."

She said quickly, "I doubt you do. We love one another, but he's married. He is also very prominent..." She allowed her words to trail off.

Samuels was stunned. *How could a prominent man allow his child's mother to live in so humble a home?*

Nenita must have read his mind. "He has offered to move me; build me a house in America, with high ceilings and manicured lawns." Her eyes flashed, and she looked away. "I don't want that from him. I have never wanted that." She turned to Samuels, her dark eyes gleaming from inside their hollow shell. "It is important that I stay here. It is also important that I take nothing from him."

Why? Samuels wondered, but he simply nodded.

"He does provide a caregiver to help me through the day." She sighed. "I can barely get along without her now, I'm afraid." She looked up, her eyes brighter. "She just left. Her name is Anna. She takes very good care of me."

Samuels smiled warmly. "It is good to have someone to take care of us."

She nodded and looked away.

He cleared his throat. "You know, it was almost by accident that I learned Mark's...true identity."

She looked at him and frowned. "I'm not sure what you mean."

Samuels tried to place the woman's accent. It was unique; a combination of Spanish and Chinese. It was actually quite pleasant as she spoke in quick, abridged phrases. She looked at him with those dark eyes and he appreciated an elegance that he hadn't noticed at first. The way she held herself, the manner in which she spoke. It was clear that, at one time, she had been a refined woman. Whatever had happened to her, whatever ill-fated misfortune was claiming her life...she deserved to know the truth about her child. He said, "Your son...sometimes thinks he is someone else."

She frowned. "Someone else?"

"Yes. It's called dissociative identity disorder. He thinks he is a man by the name of Mark Justice."

She laughed bitterly. "Mark *Justice?* That's ironic, don't you think?"

Samuels sat silently. "I'm sorry, Madam, I don't see the humor."

"My son is anything but just. He should be Mark *In*justice." Her pursed lips had begun to quiver.

"Actually, Madam, Mark Justice is a very successful private investigator. He's even done some work for Scotland Yard."

Her eyes widened, and then she shook her head. "That's absurd."

"It's true. He is highly regarded among many in the upper echelons of investigative work."

For a brief moment he thought he saw a glimmer of pride. Then, abruptly, she said, "Did he tell you what else he does? In his free time?"

Samuels bowed his head. "Yes, it came out at the end. He hadn't realized it until that moment. It was a devastating bit of knowledge for him, I'm afraid."

The woman stared at Samuels, and he thought he might wilt under her glare. With a trace of sadness, she said, "Yes...that must have been difficult for him."

The two of them sat silently as the truth of the moment sunk in. She had just learned that her killer son had a separate identity...a kinder, gentler soul. And, though it didn't change who he was, it would likely have a profound impact on her ability to love him. And love him she did...in that place that only mothers possess.

She said, "Where is he now?"

"I'm afraid I don't know. I tried to get him to...a facility that could help him, but he left town before I could do so. I'm not sure what he's doing or where he's gone." The lie fell heavy in the room. Nenita simply nodded. He added, "I was hoping to learn more about him, so that when I return to London, I might be able to help him."

She chuckled sadly. "You can't help him. His father tried his hardest, and if he – a man with access to all that the world can offer – couldn't find a way to help Mark, I doubt there's much in your bag of tricks that will do any good."

"Excuse me for asking, but who *is* his father?"

The woman narrowed her eyes. "Between us?"

"Between us."

Her voice nearly a whisper, she said, "He's an American; you may have heard of him. His name is Walter Henderson."

CHAPTER 7

Beaune, France

Cobra loosened the collar of his dirty white shirt, chuckling as he looked in the rearview mirror. His mismatched eyes were on full display, the itchy blue contacts stored in a case in his backpack. He wasn't sure why he had the blasted things, only that, on occasion, he would awaken in a strange room with those blue lenses burning his eyes. But he kept them, knowing that, from time to time, it was helpful to hide his uniquely-discolored eyes. He smoothed back strands of oily black hair, which he had pulled in a ponytail, and gave a big, toothy grin. "You're such a fox, Cobra."

He looked for signs to Beaune. He knew the city was close; he had been there before, and recalled that it was about four hours southeast of Paris. He'd been driving for at least that long, and could use a break. Besides, he had a phone call to make.

His first trip to Beaune had been in 1998, just after an incident with a priest outside the Vatican. He had needed to get away quickly, and had snuck into the back of a wine truck in Rome. He had wound up ten hours later in the French city of Beaune, drunk on cabernet, pleased that he had stumbled upon the ideal sleepy town. It had been a perfect place to disappear, and he had trolled its streets for hours, looking for a thrift shop that could give him tools to change his appearance until the situation cooled down a bit. *And now, I call upon you again, my lovely Beaune.*

He came to his exit and pulled off the highway, looking for a good place to park the van. The vehicle itself was fairly nondescript, so he wasn't worried about being noticed, so much as he needed to make sure that his special cargo couldn't escape or cause a scene. He saw what looked like an abandoned gas station about a half-mile ahead and drove toward it.

He couldn't stay in Beaune long; he needed to get to Lyon before sunset. He would have preferred to have taken high-speed rail out of Paris; it was twice as fast as the highway. But it wasn't like he could carry his six-four, two-hundred-pound half-brother onto a train. And the man had been too drugged to walk. Which meant that Cobra had needed to be inventive. Fortunately, as he was stewing over his dilemma, he had looked out the window of his dingy Paris hotel room, and had spotted a delivery van stopped in the alley below. He had been pleased to see that it was an older model, which meant that it wouldn't have GPS. He had run downstairs and had spotted the driver unloading crates at a store across the alley. Grabbing a hotel luggage cart from the basement, he had hauled it to his room using the service elevator. He had wrapped Martin in a bedspread and had rolled him onto the cart. He had stuffed his belongings in his backpack, had thrown it over his shoulder, and had rolled the luggage cart to the door. He had opened the door cautiously, and, when he was sure that no one was in the hall, he had rolled the cart to the service elevator. He had taken it to the basement, which had an access door abutting the alley. He had spotted the driver unloading the last crate from a hydraulic dolly onto the porch of a nearby shop, and had waited for him to walk back to the van. Cobra had picked up a random brick from the alley and, when the driver had reached the back of the van, he had come up from behind and had slammed the brick against the man's head. The driver had fallen to the street, and Cobra had rifled through his pockets for the keys. He had shoved the man into a drainage ditch and, using the hydraulic dolly, had hoisted Martin's wrapped body into the back of the van. He had locked the door, had run to the front, and had slid behind the wheel. He had sped from the alley to the main road, then onto the highway. When he was about twenty miles outside Paris, he had pulled off the highway to check on his passenger. Though Martin was still out cold, Cobra had gone ahead and given him another shot of morphine...*just in case.*

That was about four hours ago. He guessed the morphine would still be working, but needed to be sure. He pulled into the vacant gas station lot and parked behind an old shed. He stepped out, pulled his gun from his coat, and walked to the back of the van. He unlocked the door and, with his gun ready, he looked inside. The bundled-up Martin hadn't moved. Cobra waited another minute, but saw nothing more than the rhythmic rise and fall of the blanket. He closed and locked the door.

He looked around; the city of Beaune was less than a mile away. He tucked the gun in his pocket and set out for town, invigorated as he strolled the wide, tree-lined road. The air was crisp and clear, and again, Cobra pondered a move from the UK. France had so much more to offer than the dirty streets of London. Not only that; the man who had visited him two nights ago, the ghost who had referred to himself as Justice, had spoken with an undeniable British accent, which meant that leaving London might give Cobra a bit of distance from the haughty specter.

He flinched and picked up his pace. Justice had said things that had troubled Cobra. He had spoken of a little boy, *"...that we share inside us,"* and had suggested that even if he wanted to, Justice couldn't leave Cobra any more than Cobra could leave Justice. What did that mean? And where had Justice come from? He had sprung up so quickly...as if out of nowhere. Was he a figment of Cobra's imagination? Perhaps the result of heartburn, much like Scrooge's undigested bit of beef?

He thought again of the child...the young boy that Justice had referenced. Cobra knew Mark; he knew him well, as a matter of fact. He wasn't sure *how* he knew him, only that the child had somehow *created* Cobra from the depths of his own despair. But he had never thought of them as being one and the same. The child had *summoned* Cobra; he hadn't *become* Cobra...had he? But as he thought of it now, he realized that whenever he thought of the boy, he thought of himself, and almost always, had to fight not to cry. So, who was he? Who was Mark Villamor? And how were they related? He bristled. *That boy was the bastard child of my father, Walter.* Which was odd, because Cobra was also the bastard child of his father, Walter. But Cobra couldn't be Mark; Cobra was the boy's savior...his Superman...his King Arthur. Separate but equal, perhaps? Regardless of their genetic tie, one thing was clear: they both shared a deep-seated loathing for their father, Walter.

He put a hand to his temple; he could feel a headache coming on. *Don't think about it, Cobra.*

He continued to stroll, but quickly lost sight of his surroundings as he was overcome by memories of the day when the boy, Mark Villamor, found his voice. That day when he finally fought back...that cool day in January, when the child finally found a savior. Cobra had come about in an instant. He had entered the room like a tempest, stirring up fear in a man who had stirred up something far deeper for far too long. It had brought him utter joy to hear Kilroy, the headmaster, beg for his life. Cobra chuckled as he recalled what had happened next. He had beaten the old man senseless, freeing Mark not only of the man's filth, but of whatever place he held in the boy's damaged psyche. Then, rather than kill the man, Cobra had ended the assault by promising Kilroy that if he told anyone, Cobra would kill him in his sleep.

He had terrorized the old man for the next three years, coming and going with the ease of a summer storm. By the time he was sixteen, he had completely taken over for Mark. Any dealings with the headmaster took place with Cobra, not with the boy. Cobra had no idea where the child had gone, but it didn't matter. Cobra had freed him, and – in the process – had learned the value of inciting fear in his victims. It hadn't taken long for him to finally finish off the old headmaster, after which, he concluded that he had outgrown the school and the city of Baclayon. But, before he was able to get away from the godforsaken town, his father had had him 'put away.'

But not for long, he thought with a sneer. He had escaped the institution in a rather colorful fashion, starting a fire that had eventually taken down the building and everyone in it. He had then left the Philippines, ready for greener pastures. But there had been one thing that he had needed to do before he moved on with his life; he had needed to see his father. Not in the humble cottage where his mother lived in Baclayon, but in Walter Henderson's *real* home. So, he had left Baclayon on a quest to reclaim his and Mark's birthright. He had traveled to America, and it was there that he had begun to understand just how wronged he had been...

...It was sunset when Mark's plane touched down in Boston's Logan International. Though he was only eighteen, he looked more like twenty-five, and acted closer to thirty. Yes, Mark was an old soul. His life had started as a betrayal and a lie and he had learned much in his eighteen years. But now he had come to set the record straight...to take his rightful place in the esteemed Henderson hierarchy.

As he stepped from the plane, a brisk January wind chilled him to the bone. Except for a trip to France when he was a boy, he had never left Baclayon, the beachside prison of his youth. It was his mother who had initially wanted him to go to the boarding school just outside the city; she had grown tired of his dark moods and fitful behaviors. But it was his father, Walter, who had taken him there, locked him inside, then walked away as if he had just taken Fido to the kennel. The man had more or less washed his hands of the boy from then on. 'You ass!' he thought, as he pulled his collar tighter around his neck.

He walked into the terminal and, after a winding journey through the huge airport, he reached the front door. He stepped outside, shivering as the cold Boston wind swept through him. He pulled out a slip of paper. "4520 Kings Drive." Even the road the man lived on was pretentious. He waved down a taxi and slid in back. He gave the driver the address, then sat back, awed as he looked out the window. He had never seen such pandemonium. Baclayon had been so calm, so serene. 'Too calm,' he thought. He had needed a change, and Boston was proving to be a good start.

As they drove north on highway 93, he looked to his east and saw a large body of water. 'Cape Cod Bay,' he thought to himself; he had done his homework. He rolled down his window, hoping to smell the ocean, wanting to feel the soothing spray of the sea. But instead of the warm breezes from the Celebes, this air was bitterly cold. Even so, he smiled, calmed by the sounds and smells that had saved him so many times in the past.

"Hey! Shut that window, you idiot!"

Cobra glared at the driver as he rolled up the window, suppressing an urge to choke the man. He watched the buildings of downtown gradually change to groomed lawns and city parks, and soon saw the lofty gates that guarded the grand mansions of Boston. 'The family has done well,' he thought with a scowl. The cab slowed and stopped in front of a tall gate.

"Can't go any further, pal."

Cobra stepped out of the cab and looked up at a small sign to the side of the gate. 'No admittance' was etched in scrolled letters, and he could feel the anger surge inside him. Those two words seemed to apply to Mark's entire life. He threw a fifty-dollar bill at the driver, then stood at the gate as the cab pulled away. "No admittance, my ass." He looked around and, seeing only one security camera and no armed guards, he reached up, disabled the camera, and scaled the six-foot fence with ease. He walked several hundred yards along a paved drive, staying close to the tree line in case someone was monitoring the grounds. He stopped in front of a massive brick mansion with tall white pillars, ornate statues, and a perfectly-groomed lawn. He smoothed down his corduroy jacket, adjusted his tie, and ran his fingers through his long black hair. He stared at the stately manor, thinking of all he had been denied; the luxuries and prestige that should have been his. He trembled as he stood silent and still, a statue among so many. He cleared his throat and wiped his hands on his pants. 'I'll walk up those steps and knock on those double doors with the pride of ownership...my ownership...as a son of the esteemed Walter Henderson. "Daddy, I'm home." ' He chuckled nervously as he climbed the stairs, ready to stake his claim.

Before he had reached the second stair, a man dressed in black appeared at the door. His face was stern as he eyed the boy who had somehow gotten past the gate. Behind him, hidden in the shadow of a massive foyer, were two men holding guns. He heard footsteps, and turned to see another man aiming a rifle at the back of his head. The man who had answered the door narrowed his eyes. "May I help you?"

Cobra said evenly, 'Is Mr. Henderson here?'

The man frowned. 'May I tell him who's calling?'

Cobra paused. Who's calling? His son? His worst nightmare? He had to hide a chuckle. "Yes, please tell him Nenita Villamor's son has come to see him."

The man turned and walked inside, leaving Cobra at the door with the two armed guards not far away. He heard the guard behind him cock his rifle. Cobra turned to face him. He walked down the steps and was about to confront the man, when he heard the front door open. He looked over his shoulder, disgusted at the admiration he couldn't help but feel for his father's eminence. Walter was dignified in every way; even the simple act of walking across the portico revealed his remarkable presence. He came down the steps, waving away the guard who had cocked the gun, but saying nothing to the two guards who had walked out behind him. He stopped within inches of Cobra, his blue eyes flashing. "What do you want?"

Cobra tightened his jaw. "What do I want?" He smiled coolly. "Why, Daddy, I've come home."

Walter took Cobra by the arm and walked him to a bench off to the side of the house, motioning for the armed guards to stay put. He leaned close to Cobra and whispered sternly, "This isn't your home."

Cobra glared at him. He was tempted to shout the next few words, but out of some odd deference for the man he hated, he whispered, as well. "No, you're right. My home is a hovel. Does my mother know how you live in your 'other life?' Is she aware of the riches you possess with your...wife?"

Walter bristled. "Actually, she is. Your mother is ill, Mark. Why aren't you down there with her?"

"I'm never going back there. Baclayon isn't big enough for my...appetites."

Walter flinched, a hint of fear visible in his normally commanding eyes. "How did you get out of...the facility?"

"You mean the insane asylum?" He laughed. "I...uh...created a diversion."

Walter's jaw tightened. "I see. So, I'll ask again, what do you want, Mark?"

Cobra chuckled. "Justice. I want justice, Daddy..."

Cobra bristled as he smoothed back strands of black hair. Not much had come of that visit. He had left Boston without incident, but the memory of that house, the statues, the forbidding gate...had left an indelible impression. *There's much I don't have; most of it I don't need. But I do require a reprisal that is just...and concrete.*

A passerby suddenly tripped, spilling coffee on Cobra's grey suit. *"Pardonnez-moi, monsieur."*

Cobra scowled. "Imbecile!"

The man hurried away as Cobra stood and wiped the coffee from his shirt and his jacket lapel. He was still wearing the gray suit he had bought from the store on the Rue de Lille two nights earlier; it was wrinkled, and now it was stained.

I need new clothes. He chuckled; he knew just the place to go. He had reached the city's downtown, and he turned left on the first side street. He turned left again down an alley that led to a row of old shops. He walked up to a rusted door that was hanging askew, opened it, and walked inside. An old woman was seated behind the counter. She, like the counter, had seen better days. He recognized her. *The question is, does she recognize me?* He had visited the shop years ago after his trip to the Vatican, when he had also needed a change of clothes. The woman had been in the same spot...*she might have been wearing the same dress.* She looked up from a stack of books and was about to say something when she stopped. She quickly lowered her eyes. He grinned as he walked past her to the back of the store. He scanned racks of clothes, nodding when he saw what he wanted. *The French National Police...perfect.*

He bought the uniform, making sure to include a hat. As he left the shop, a bell rang out two chimes. *Two o'clock in France...which means it's eight p.m. in Baclayon.* He closed his eyes and leaned against the side of an old building. He could almost hear the waves hitting the coastline...smell the saltwater in the air...see the yellow-orange of the setting sun as the boats tied up for the night. And he could feel the emptiness of a little boy going to his dormitory room...alone.

He opened his eyes and frowned. *It's time for me to make that call.*

CHAPTER 8

Lyon, France

Maddi smoothed wrinkles from her jacket – Henderson's jacket – then rubbed her tired eyes. She had napped on the train, but it wasn't nearly enough. They had arrived in Lyon just moments ago, and, as they walked from the train to the station, she could feel the fatigue overtaking her. She ran her fingers through her shoulder-length blonde hair, thinking how good it would feel to soak in a hot tub. But a bath would have to wait, as would the unfettered sleep that had been calling to her for days now. Cobra had taken Henderson, and, though Henderson's text suggested that he had escaped, she knew it was too soon to celebrate.

She and Brooks followed Seacroft to the front of the terminal, where they were to meet up with a friend of Seacroft's. Within seconds, a blue Audi pulled up and a heavyset man stepped from the car. Seacroft shook his hand, then turned to her and Brooks. "This is Ethan Bouton, an old friend whom we can trust with our lives."

Bouton was short and wide with a welcoming smile, and he gave a quick nod as he helped the three of them stuff their bags in the trunk. Brooks and Maddi sat in back, while Seacroft sat in the front passenger seat. Bouton left the terminal and sped through the busy streets of Lyon.

Seacroft said to him, "Have the guys checked out the hotel?"

Ethan nodded. "Yes. Everything is ready."

"How far away?"

"Twenty minutes."

Maddi checked her watch impatiently. She had gotten Henderson's text over five hours ago. What had happened since? Was he safe in a hotel room in downtown Lyon? Or was he in trouble, with Cobra just minutes away from taking him again?

She said nothing as they drove through downtown Lyon. Though bigger than she had expected, it still held the charm of a European village...and it felt deceiving. Henderson was out there, somewhere, hiding...in fear of his life...yet tourists and city-dwellers alike strolled the streets without a care in the world...*as if a maniac isn't on the loose and could take them at any moment.*

They reached the hotel, and Seacroft helped her out of the car. They grabbed their bags from the trunk, and Bouton led them through the front door of the Hotel le Royal. Seacroft walked to the desk and checked in, proffering their passports in exchange for two keys to the suite. He led the way to the elevator, and they took it to the fifth floor. They stepped off and walked to their suite. Though Bouton had assured Seacroft that the room had been inspected and was clear, Seacroft checked it anyway. Maddi waited impatiently. Seacroft waved them in just as a mantel clock struck a single chime. It was two-fifteen. Brooks tipped the bellman, and carried the bags into their rooms. When she could stand it no longer, Maddi said, "It's been over six hours. We need to find Matt."

Seacroft frowned. "First, I need to call the boss." He pulled out his phone.

Maddi took him by the arm and looked at him pleadingly. "Can't it wait...I'm pretty sure that time is of the essence."

Seacroft hesitated, then sighed. "Okay. I'll call from the square." He shoved the phone in his pocket. "Where did Matt say to meet?"

"He didn't. He simply wrote 'Place Bellecour.'"

Seacroft frowned. "We'll get a cup of coffee and wait at one of the tables in the square." He paused. "Maddi, you need to stay close to us; it's a wide-open space."

She nodded and grabbed her purse. She spotted Henderson's journal in one of the pockets. "Give me a minute, Spencer." Whatever Henderson had written in that journal wasn't meant for others to see. She took it from her purse and walked it to the safe in the master bedroom. She made up a password and locked it inside.

She went back to the desk, grabbed her purse, and, at the last minute, picked up the red scarf that her brother Andrew had given her a few Christmases ago. She smiled as she draped it around her neck. *"So I can find you in a crowd,"* he told her at the time.

They walked out of the suite, went to the elevator, and took it to the lobby. They left the hotel and walked two blocks to the square. Maddi was surprised to see people everywhere. If Henderson was trying to escape Cobra, why would he have her meet him in such a public place? Then again, what could go wrong with people all around? *A lot,* she thought, as she recalled the murder of the Secretary of State at the Queen's Ball. They walked through the square, and a cool but pleasant breeze blew her hair in her eyes. As she brushed it away, she shivered, but not from the wind. *Yes, a lot can happen in the company of strangers.*

CHAPTER 9

Baclayon, in the Philippines

I'm so tired. Nenita had done her best to make her guest feel welcome, but she knew she would pay for it when he left. The simple act of putting on a kind face and pouring a glass of water had taken its toll, let alone the news that her wicked son had a side to him that wasn't wicked; that her love for him could be justified by an alter ego named Justice.

She had made every effort to be kind to the man sitting in the chair across from her; after all, he had traveled quite a distance to try to help her son. She had focused on his every word, trying to understand what he was telling her; what it was that had compelled him to fly half-way around the world to find her. She had barely noticed the daylight leaving and the darkness sneaking in.

As the shadows had overtaken them, she had switched on a lamp, listening intently as Samuels spoke of the intricacies of "Split Personality." She had paid close attention as he went through the various psychological responses that could bring about such a thing. Though she had wanted to crawl to her bed and relinquish her soul to the comfort of sleep, she had forced herself to stay focused as he told her of her son; not the cold-blooded killer that the world knew as Cobra, but a respected detective known ironically as Justice. She had wanted to cry with joy, even though she knew that Justice was an imposter. But for a brief few moments, she had a son she could be proud of. Why couldn't he stay; why couldn't the respected investigator choose that persona over the killer who had shamed her all these years? She had wanted to ask the doctor all those questions and more, but had been too weak to do anything but listen.

The more Samuels talked, the more it seemed as if he was speaking from a distance; as if she was seeing his image from far away, not across from her in her living room. She was afraid she might pass out, which she did often now, the cancer having taken over most of her body the past year. It had left her weak, pieces of her disappearing a little at a time. But she made herself listen; she needed to hear the words of this man who seemed to actually be *fond* of her son. It gave her energy to hear him ache for Mark's tragedy and express anger over the poor boy's injustices. How many times had she prayed that Mark would find redemption; a life filled with purpose and kind deeds?

"If I may ask, Madam, at what point did you know the truth about your son?"

She looked at Samuels, then closed her eyes, refusing to say a word as she recalled the moment when she realized that Mark was the killer known as Cobra. It was Walter who had forced her to see it...to face the monster they had created...

"You have to look, Nenita."

"I don't want to."

"I know. And I don't want to show you... but you have to know the truth."

Nenita turned and looked at him, her eyes wounded, her heart heavy. "Why?"

"Because, Nenita, he's ours."

"No, it can't be. Please, Walter, don't make me look."

Walter held her tight. "Nenita, it's him. Look..."

Nenita turned her eyes to the photo – in color – that was placed at the top of the article, "Cobra kills a priest." She looked past the stringy black hair, the hollow cheeks with their carved lines of anger and hate. She went straight to the eyes; the two eyes so different from one another, yet

somehow similar to the man who was hugging her now.
They possessed a hint of magic...like Walter's. But they were
so much darker; so much less enlightened than the man she
had loved for the past twenty years.

She couldn't turn away. She had seen those eyes a
thousand times, but had allowed herself to ignore the truth.
As she stared at them now, there was no denying it; the
brutal murderer known as Cobra was their little boy, their
Mark...

Nenita had barely recovered from it, finally coming to
terms with the fact that a spark of evil can arise from
anywhere. Though she hadn't lived a sin-free life, she had
never intentionally hurt another soul. As for Walter; he was
nearly perfect. He was kind, gifted, and honorable. But
somehow, the two of them had created a killer.

But this Dr. Samuels has seen a good man.

"I'd rather not say," she said, in reply to his question.
Gathering her strength, she said, "Tell me, Dr. Samuels. What
does he look like? When he's Justice, I mean."

Samuels smiled. "Quite respectable, Madam. He has
shoulder-length blond hair and engaging blue eyes, and his
smile is as gracious as any I have ever seen."

In spite of her best efforts, Nenita began to cry. She
quickly wiped away the tears, angry for allowing herself to
break down. She nodded, unable to say anything more. But
there was so much she wanted to ask; so much she wanted to
put into her head instead of the rotten images that had filled
it for so long. She was about to ask about the office where her
son worked when a phone rang from the kitchen. She was
startled by it; the phone rang so rarely. "Ex—Excuse me," she
managed to say as she rose from her chair. Her gait was slow,
her weakness magnified by the faded robe that seemed to

swallow her whole as she walked into the kitchen. She was out of breath as she lifted the receiver. "Hello?"

"Hi Nenita. It's your loving son, Mark. I was wondering...would you like to come to a party?"

CHAPTER 10

Baclayon, in the Philippines

Samuels watched Nenita as she walked to the kitchen. Her robe was like an oversized suit of armor, clinging awkwardly as it held off the slings and arrows of a troubled life. He waited, sipping his water, taking in the décor of her simple home outside Baclayon. The darkness had descended, shrouding the furniture and the worn carpet in shades of gray. There was a warmth to the old table and chairs, a comfort in the threadbare rug, an easiness to the frayed wallpaper. The place didn't feel cold or sterile; it felt welcoming...even homey. Which made it seem like an odd place for Mark to have grown up. Samuels had expected a hellhole, but instead he had found a house filled with humility and grace.

He glanced at his watch. *Eight-thirty p.m. here...one-thirty in the afternoon in the UK.* He had been travelling since seven the night before, and felt certain that if he didn't get up from that chair, he would fall asleep.

He stood and walked out to the hallway. He suddenly remembered that he had asked the cab driver to wait for him, and opened the door. The cab was gone. Samuels couldn't blame the man. It had been over an hour since he had arrived at the house. *I suppose I can call him when I need him.* He closed the door and turned to look at a picture that he had noticed when he had walked in; a photo of Nenita with Mark, who must have been only four or five at the time, along with a man whom Samuels now assumed was Walter Henderson. He looked closely at the picture, admiring Nenita's beauty; she had still been healthy then, with strong cheekbones and bright eyes. Her wrists were turned down, and Samuels wondered if the cuts he had seen earlier had been made after the picture or before.

Young Mark was sitting on her lap and, at first glance, he, too, seemed vibrant and alive. His smile was genuine, two teeth absent in front, chubby cheeks bunched like marshmallows on each side of a wide grin. But, as Samuels looked closer, he could see darkness in the oddly-colored eyes. It was clear his troubles had already begun. Mark had taken that first step over the line that separated sanity and insanity. *Was he born that way? Did evil rise up within him, like black oil that had sat waiting, biding its time, bubbling beneath the earth? Or was it beaten into him...like a scar.*

He continued his scrutiny. Walter, broad-shouldered and strikingly handsome, was sitting on the other side of Mark, his one hand resting gently on Mark's shoulder, the other clasping Nenita's delicate bronze fingers as they rested on Mark's lap. But his eyes were revealing, as well. This arrangement wasn't comfortable for him...and why would it be? According to Nenita, he was the overseer of a powerful dynasty. What business did he have playing house with a simple woman from the Philippines? *He was doing this to comfort her...to give her – and their life – some semblance of legitimacy.*

Samuels looked closer. Walter's eyes were bluer than any he had ever seen; they reminded him of Justice's. And, though he knew now that Justice must have been wearing contact lenses, the similarity was uncanny.

He walked back to the living room and sat down in the chair. He had recognized Walter's name, but he couldn't recall how. It didn't matter; Walter had barely been at that home...his absence was all that was important.

Nenita hung up the phone. She stood in the kitchen, absorbing the call. She tried to think what time it would be in Europe. She glanced at a clock, but couldn't seem to do the math. She knew it must be afternoon. Where was her son when he made the call? And who was he? Justice? Or the Cobra, whose 'handiwork' had last been seen in Calais, France. He had seemed polite on the phone. Was it possible that he had returned to London as the respectable Mark Justice, and was enjoying a drink with friends after a hard day's work? *Which one of them phoned me?* she thought, as she crossed herself and whispered a quick prayer.

She pulled the robe more tightly around her and walked out to the sitting room. The call from her son had unnerved her. He hadn't called in years; the last time had been four years ago, when the men from America had come to visit her. She hadn't known them, but they had told her that they had an offer for Mark, and, if she was cooperative, it would help him 'overcome' his troubles. All she had needed to do was tell him that they hadn't hurt her when he called. She had talked to him only briefly; they had little to discuss. What do you say to your son, the killer?

Though she knew she shouldn't, she wanted to honor her son's request. She wanted to go to him. She wanted to see him one last time. And, just maybe, he would show her a glimpse of the man that Dr. Samuels had described...the respectable Mark Justice. *And then I can die knowing that at least a part of his life is spent doing good.*

She looked at Samuels sitting in the chair. With his beard and his three-piece suit, he could have been a kind uncle, or even a priest. Should she tell him what had just happened? After all, it was her son he had come to see her about. And, if she decided to go, she knew she couldn't make the trip alone.

She walked to the chair and looked down at the doctor's kind eyes. "A remarkable thing has just occurred, Doctor. That call was from...Mark. He says he wants me to join him...for a party."

Samuels had been reaching for his water when Nenita walked in from the kitchen. He was about to take a drink, when she made her pronouncement. He set the glass on the table. Doing his best to sound calm, he said, "I see. And are you going?"

She nodded. "I'd like to. I'd like to see him one more time before I...die."

Samuels nodded solemnly. "Did he tell you where to meet him?"

"Only that there will be a plane waiting for me in Baclayon first thing in the morning." She paused. "He cautioned me that the flight would take nearly a full day."

Samuels nodded. He was well aware.

She took a deep breath, then said quietly, "Would you like to come with me?"

Samuels had to hide his surprise. It was the redemption that he himself had been seeking. A chance to either save – or kill – the Cobra. He cleared his throat and, against his better judgment, said, "Why, yes, I'd love to."

She nodded. "Good. I don't think I can make the trip alone."

Samuels had to agree; even since the call, she seemed to have weakened a bit more. He would go with her and take the opportunity to see Mark again; perhaps he could even convince him to come back to London, which would give Samuels a chance to prepare Scotland Yard. He nodded. "I'll need to secure a seat on the flight."

She frowned. "That's the odd thing, Doctor. He said there were two tickets."

Samuels' eyes widened. *Did he have me followed?* How had he known she would have a companion? Suddenly he felt hopeful. *He traced my steps...because he wants my help.* "He said the flight leaves in the morning?"

She nodded. "Eight a.m." She added, "you're welcome to sleep on the couch."

He smiled. "That would be quite suitable. Thank you."

She hesitated, then said quietly, "Would you like to see Mark's bedroom?" She frowned. "I've...I've done nothing to it since he left."

Again, Samuels had to hide his surprise. He guessed Justice to be around thirty. He had no idea when the boy, Mark, went to the boarding school, but he had likely been no older than twelve. *Nearly twenty years...and she hasn't touched the room?* He smiled. "I would love to see it."

She led him to a hallway, then walked to a closed door at the end of the hall. "In there," she said, and pointed at the door. "I'll wait out here."

Samuels opened the door and stepped inside, quickly closing the door behind him. He was instantly swallowed by one singular sensation: loneliness. The room was plain, with little to show of a boy's joyful curiosity. No baseballs, no marbles, no Manny Pacquiao poster on the wall. Nothing but a bed, a white painted wall, a wood floor. He spotted a bookcase along one wall and walked to it. He scanned the titles of the few books on the top shelf. They were telling. Sherlock Holmes, Edgar Allen Poe, the Odyssey, along with a translated copy of Dostoevsky's *"Demons."* No light reading for that boy; no Sci-fi, no comic books, just the heavy tomes of dark writers.

On the shelf below was an array of old coins. Secured in protective sleeves, the coins were neatly organized by year, a printed tag under each one. Samuels put a hand to his vest pocket where his own coin – the coin given to him by his father – was kept. He took it out and held it tenderly, rubbing his fingers over the coarse cold metal. Suddenly overcome, he slid the coin in his pocket and loosened his collar. *I am here not to recall my own past, but the past of the man I have come to save.*

He tugged at his beard, recalling his first visit with Justice, when the anxious young man had taken a moment to look past his fears and offer a comment on Samuels' coin...

Mark shifted nervously and tapped his fingers on the desk. Suddenly he pointed to the coin by Samuels' ledger. "Now, isn't that a fascinating relic."

"Yes, it's from my father."

Mark nodded. "A silver shekel...from Israel's First Revolt...in 66 A.D., if I'm not mistaken."

Samuels' eyes widened. "You know your coins."

Mark cleared his throat. "Something I learned as a boy."

"I see. Please, tell me more."

Mark shook his head. "I'd rather not."

Samuels frowned as he stared at the neatly-arranged coins. There was no doubt about it; their presence was telling.

"Mark's father introduced him to the coins."

Samuels looked over his shoulder, surprised to see Nenita standing at the door. She was visibly shaking, and he wondered how long it had been since she had actually laid eyes on the room. He nodded and smiled. "It's quite a collection."

She sighed. "Yes. They did have a bit of fun with it." She leaned against the doorjamb, smiling wistfully. "You know, Doctor, this was a far lovelier room...at one time."

Samuels' eyes widened. "Really? Please, tell me more."

Her eyes brightened. "Mark's father, when he learned of the boy, he poured so much magic into this room." She paused, the memory clearly painful, yet comforting. "Colorful wallpaper, cheery drapes...and a charming little desk that sat over there." She pointed to an empty corner, staring as if she expected to see the desk – and the child – devoted to some fantastical boyhood scheme. "There were children's books in the bookcase, pictures on the walls, and a turntable with a collection of such happy records." She smiled; it was genuine in spite of tears that had escaped her dark eyes.

Though Samuels didn't want to pressure the poor woman, he couldn't help but ask, "What happened to the books, the pictures...the magic?"

She sighed. "Something...took hold of Mark. I don't know what it was...well, I can guess, but nonetheless, soon after his twelfth birthday, in the middle of the night he took all of it, piece by piece, into the backyard," her voice lowered to a whisper, "...and he set a match to it."

Samuels was unable to hide his shock. "He *burned* it...all of it?"

She nodded, her agony hanging heavy in the room. "Except for the bookcase."

Samuels shook his head. It occurred to him as he looked around that bleak and empty chamber, that he was seeing the aftermath of a young boy's turmoil, a child's rage frozen in time. *As if I'm looking at a fossil of a future killer's fury.* He simply stared at Nenita. There were no words to express the empathy he felt for this mother who had witnessed the demise of her child – her son – before her very eyes.

He was about to leave, when he spotted a scrapbook on the bottom shelf of the bookcase. He knelt and put a hand to the cover. He said over his shoulder, "May I?'

Nenita sighed; a deep lament that ran through her entire body. She nodded.

Samuels pulled the scrapbook from the shelf and laid it on the floor. It was standard size, not too thick, with a blank cover. He opened it and was met with a full-page color photo of the boy, Mark. He looked to be about nine or ten. Olive-skinned like his mother, his features were characteristic of his Filipino heritage. But the most notable feature was the eyes, their disparity obvious, one eye black, the other gray. What was less obvious was what lay beyond them. But Samuels could see it; he could see the dark emptiness that so often typifies the psychotic mind. As if he was looking into a chasm; an unending abyss that – if the observer isn't careful – can pull him all the way to hell. The smile confirmed it; it wasn't the innocent smile of a happy child, but the ominous sneer of a madman-to-be. Now it was clear; whatever had happened in that boarding school was bad, but the seeds had been planted long before.

He turned the page, and was surprised to see a newspaper article. The next page also had an article, as did the next and the one after it. The headlines read like a police blotter: "Child Abducted from his Manila Home;" "Stalker on the Loose after Attack on Woman in Baclayon." Page after page of horror and violence. Samuels turned to ask Nenita about them. She was gone. What must she have thought as her child immortalized such items in his scrapbook? Or when he chose Poe over Carroll, Homer over Lewis? It was hard to say, but one thing was clear. That room wasn't the bedroom of a happy boy. No, it was an inside look at a killer in the making.

Samuels was about to return the scrapbook to the shelf, when he noticed several clippings in the back. They hadn't made it to the plastic-covered pages, but their presence was every bit as telling. He laid them out in front of him, then held up the first article. "Humanitarian Father Passes Legacy to Famous Son." There was a photo captioned, "Jeremy Henderson with son Walter." Samuels skimmed the article, the last line revealing the noble heritage that had been bestowed upon the family. *"Entrusted with the task of keeping Latvia free of Soviet Russia, the Hendersons have carved their legacy into the hearts and minds of the Latvian people."*

There were several more articles, all of them filled with photos and stories of Walter with his parents at their stately home in Boston, with friends at Harvard in the spring of '52, on luxury yachts, at debutante balls, or behind the scenes with his father in Eisenhower's White House. One article told of his wedding to Dora McGregor, the highly regarded daughter of Samuel McGregor of New Haven. Another showcased the birth of their son, Martin. "The Hope for the Next Generation," read the headline. There was nothing in the article about Nenita, or about Walter's other son, and Samuels winced as he imagined young Mark Villamor trying to make sense of it.

He pulled out the final article and held it up. Taken from a magazine, it was in color and showed a photo of a man, Walter, with his hand resting on the shoulder of a boy holding a trophy. That blond-haired, blue-eyed boy wasn't Mark, and Samuels' heart ached for the moment when Mark finally put it all together...when he finally took note of a life he could have had, but never would.

He was about to return the articles to the scrapbook, when he noticed that a few of them had cut-outs pasted onto the photos. He choked as he saw an image of a boy – the same boy who was on the first page – pasted next to Walter and Martin, as if he actually belonged. There were three such inserts, and beneath the last was a poem...

"How alone can one boy feel
When left to watch as others claim
A life he knows is all too real

Except to him, his father's shame.
He dwells a lot on death, they say
But how could he not see it's gleam
When death alone gives him a way
To silence his eternal scream."

Samuels gasped, his understanding of the boy, Mark, taking on an entirely new perspective. Not only had the boy been left behind by circumstance, but he had nursed a grievance that had surely scalded his very soul.

Samuels was shaking as he placed the clippings in the scrapbook and returned it to the shelf. He rose slowly, emitting a sigh as he looked at it lying haplessly among the few items that actually mattered. Had Nenita ever seen it? He felt that she had, but he guessed that Walter had not. Samuels tried to imagine the agony the man would feel were he to learn of his son's despair at having been left behind in such a way. He wondered how Mark had come across the articles. It had to have been unsettling. Not only to find them, but to read them, and then preserve them as constant reminders of how life had failed him. *A labor not of love, but of longing.*

Samuels took another look around. For whatever reason, he didn't want to leave. He spotted a door – a closet? – and walked over to it. He opened it and looked inside. There was a pair of pants, two shirts, and a pair of shoes. That was it. No boxes filled with toys or old books; no hats or boots or trophies. He closed the door and leaned against it as he took one last look at the stark room. *So much sorrow lies dormant here.* He sighed, then walked out, closing the door behind him.

Nenita was standing in the hallway. He cleared his throat and said quickly, "Thank you for showing me his room, Nenita. It was helpful."

She said nothing, simply opening a nearby closet and pulling out a pillow and blanket. She carried the items to the couch, then said softly, "Will this do, Doctor?"

He smiled. "Yes, it's perfect." She turned and walked to her room. He followed her, stopping outside the door. "Can you pack without help?"

She nodded. "I believe I can. I seem to have a bit more energy. I'll call Anna in the morning and tell her not to come for a few days."

She disappeared into her room. He watched her with admiration. He didn't know her story, but was looking forward to hearing it.

As he walked to the sitting room, he stopped at a window that looked out at a patch of overgrown grass toward the back of the house. There were weeds throughout, but in the forgiving light of the moon, he could imagine a beautiful garden. Had that ever been the case? Had the garden, like Nenita, been vibrant and lovely not so long ago? He looked past the plot of grass for a swing set or a sandbox, something to show that a child had once lived there; there was nothing. Had those items been there at one time? *What was it like growing up here?*

He shook his head. *It doesn't matter.* That backyard had little to do with what had happened to Mark Villamor. The seeds of his upbringing had been imbedded in infancy, then emboldened in a seared and soulless bedroom. They had been memorialized in a scrapbook filled with hope...and hate. Fed with envy, watered with solitude, and pruned in the cold hallways of a sterile boarding school, the poor lad had been reared by a headmaster who, from what Justice had told him, had been capable of the worst kind of evil. *Terror upon terror...sin upon sin.*

But why had Mark been sent there? Had he been incorrigible from the start? The result of some genetic mishap, perhaps? And why had Walter and Nenita chosen the boarding school outside Baclayon? Had there been no other schools to choose from? How much had they known about what had gone on at that school? Surely, they weren't aware of what was happening to their young boy...right? Those questions and more he would ask Nenita as they made the long trip to see Mark. *And perhaps, together, we can bring him home.*

CHAPTER 11

Lyon, Paris,

Martin Henderson massaged his temples, the ache in his head overpowering every one of his senses. *Where am I?* He rubbed his shoulder, wincing as he opened one eye and looked around. He was in a square room with a dirt floor and a high ceiling, and the only light was coming from a window high on one wall. *Is it morning?* he wondered. He couldn't tell from the angle of the light. He had come awake just minutes ago, aware only that he had been shoved to the ground. He recalled trying to fight back, and that he had been unable to even lift his arms.

He tried to sit up, but was forced back down by the headache. He squeezed his temples, trying to push away the pain. *What happened to me?* He closed his eyes, trying to remember. He and Hank Clarkson had gone looking for Hank's CIA son, Roger, who had been taken by Cobra and was being held in a cave beneath Paris. They had found him on the verge of death, and Henderson had compelled Cobra to leave Roger and take him, instead. He had then been drugged and brought...where? *To a hotel.* Again, he opened his eyes and looked around. Clearly, he was no longer in a hotel. The room was cold and damp, with no furnishings other than a rusted chamber pot along one wall. It smelled moldy...and old. *A dungeon?*

He dragged himself closer to the window, his head throbbing with even the slightest movement. He breathed in and caught a scent of pine. *Where the hell am I?* Using the stones in the wall as grips, he was able to lift his body to standing. His throat burned, and he was having a hard time getting air. He was dizzy, but forced his eyes to stay open as he hugged the wall. Though it was cold in the cell, he was sweating, a salty droplet falling onto the edge of his mouth. He licked it away. He guessed the room to be about ten feet square. The only window was about four feet above him, and it had three metal bars blocking anyone from climbing in...or out.

Memories were coming in bits and pieces. Cobra had led him from the Paris cave to a hotel room, but what had happened next? He dug deep for the memory. *A narcotic.* Cobra had given him a shot as they were leaving the cave. *Am I still feeling its effects?* He clutched the wall as he took one unsteady step, then another. *Why didn't he just kill me?* Henderson sighed; he knew the answer. *He wants me to suffer.*

He felt a rush of cold air from the window and began to shiver. Again, the smell of pine. He looked for a chair or bench; something to climb onto to reach the bars in the window. There was nothing; the room was bare but for the chamber pot.

How long have I been here? Using one arm to hug the wall, he patted his jacket, looking for a cellphone. His pockets were empty. His stomach growled, the sound of it startling him. When had he last eaten? He licked his lips; they were dry, dryer than they should be. *What drug did that monster give me?* He felt the urge to urinate and stumbled to the chamber pot. He gripped the wall as he relieved himself. Though the urine smelled strong, there was plenty of it; he wasn't dehydrated, which meant he couldn't have been out too long. *Still Monday...maybe Tuesday at the latest.*

He leaned against the wall. He blinked, then blinked again, surprised to see a loaf of bread and two bottles of water on a pad by the door. They must have been hidden by a shadow. *Why would Cobra feed me?* He nodded. *So he can torture me.*

He lowered to his knees and crawled to the food. *What if it's poisoned?* He shook his head. *No...poison would be too quick.* He grabbed the loaf and pulled away a chunk. *I could refuse to eat...go on a hunger strike.* He frowned. Cobra wouldn't care. He would probably just stick in an IV.

He stuck the chunk of bread in his mouth, chewed it, then picked up one of the waters. He took two giant gulps, then instantly felt a cramp in his gut; his stomach wasn't ready. He leaned over and threw up all of it. *Smaller bites...smaller sips of water.* He tried again. This time he was able to keep it down.

A tower rang out in the distance; he counted the chimes. *It's 4:00 p.m.* He thought of Roger in the caves beneath Paris. Had he survived? Had Hank managed to keep him alive until Maddi got there? *Did* she get there? Was she safe? He closed his eyes, his heart aching as he thought of the woman he loved. Though it physically hurt to think of her, he couldn't stand *not* to...the way her eyes glimmered when she looked at him, how she tucked her hair behind her ear when she was deep in thought. He fell onto his side, longing to hold her one more time as the sun came up...

"So, do you like eggs in the morning? Or are you more of a coffee and toast sort of guy?"

Henderson stroked her hair. "I like a croissant with tea, actually."

She chuckled. "Of course you do."

He scooted closer. "What do you mean?"

She grinned. "While the rest of the world is eating bacon and eggs, you're buttering a croissant and steeping tea." She paused. "Don't worry; I kind of like it."

He laughed. "Why?"

"Because it fits."

He grinned. "What do you mean 'it fits.'?"

"You should eat croissants. The elegant Martin Henderson should sip tea and eat pastry."

He chuckled and shook his head. "What do you like in the morning?"

She turned to him and a strand of hair fell over one eye. She brushed it away, pulled him closer, and said, "You...."

He grabbed his chest. Would he ever look into those eyes again? Or feel her fingers on his skin? He would give anything, even his life to be with her one last time. *If I hadn't already sold my soul, Maddi, I'd sell it readily for another night with you.*

He was starting to feel lightheaded, so he closed his eyes and laid his head on the ground. The dirt was cold; it felt good. He thought again of Maddi...of the last time he had seen her. They had been telling one another goodbye from across the foyer of his family's Latvian estate. Suddenly, he panicked. What if Cobra knew of her; what if he had learned of their relationship? Using what little strength he had left, he said aloud, "You will never...get her, Cobra. I'll die before I...let you...hurt Maddi."

As though from the ether, he heard the ice-cold voice of his captor. "Too late, dear brother. She's on her way."

CHAPTER 12

Lyon, France

Cobra chuckled as he listened to his half-brother's pitiful lament. He was glad he had gotten back in time to hear it. He said louder, "Not only is she on her way, but I have something really special planned for her." He waited, but there was nothing; no sharp retort, no clever reply. "Tuckered out, old boy?" He laughed, then spun around and sat with his back against the dungeon's outside wall. His dream had come true. He had captured his half-brother, and now he was about to put the poor man through hell.

But getting him to the dungeon hadn't been easy. They had arrived in Lyon about an hour ago and Cobra had stopped the van a few hundred yards from the Basilica de Fourvière, with no idea how to get Henderson to the dungeon that sat about a mile behind it. A relic from the Inquisition, Cobra had stumbled upon the dungeon during one of his many journeys to the city. But the path to get to it consisted of fields, forests, and ravines. How could he drag an unconscious, 200-pound man back there? He had decided that the only way was to once again use the dolly. Keeping his brother wrapped in the blanket, he had rolled him out of the van and onto the dolly. He had strapped him in, and, angling the dolly level with the ground, he had dragged it through the tall grass to the ravine. Once there, he was able to move more freely, and had managed to wheel the heavy dolly around the perimeter, nearly dropping Henderson into the ravine at least three times. Once he had reached the other side, he had guided the dolly down the hill and through the creek, which was thankfully not too deep and only a few feet wide. When they were across, he had hauled the dolly through the forest, having to drag it over fallen limbs and through the thick undergrowth. When he had finally gotten to the other end of the trees, he had dragged the dolly through more tall grass to the back side of a hill. With a herculean effort, he had lugged Henderson up the hill to the dungeon. Though that dungeon was only a mile from the Basilica, it had taken him over forty minutes to get there, and by then, the man had begun to stir. Cobra had punched him in the jaw as he had unstrapped him, and had shoved him onto the dirt floor. The poor man had landed on his shoulder and had groaned, but he hadn't opened his eyes. Cobra had left bread and water, had locked the door, and had taken the blanket and dolly back to the van. He had shoved both items in the back and had driven to the edge of town, where he had wiped everything down and had left the van behind an abandoned shed. He had then hiked back to the dungeon, reaching it just in time to hear his brother's speech.

He checked the time. It was after four; he had a lot to do. *At least my poor brother won't starve.* Cobra had left water and bread for Henderson, but not just any bread. It had been bought in an Asian market near his Paris hotel. Cobra had tried to give it to him there, but Martin had been too drugged to eat. Cobra felt certain that as the morphine wore off, Martin would devour the bread. *Then, let the games begin!*

As he sat beneath the dungeon's window, he stared at the tall grass, pale green and waving with the breeze. Though it felt as if he was a hundred miles from Lyon, he was close enough to hear the sounds from the basilica; bells celebrating afternoon mass, a bus horn signaling the arrival of tourists. He grinned as he yelled up to the window. "Brother, we should go to the city and play." He flinched. "I never had anyone to play with, you know. It would've been so fun, you and me." He waited; again, no reply. He checked his watch. *Four-fifteen...I need to get back to the square.*

He brushed a strand of stringy black hair from his face as he stood and walked around the dungeon to its door. He slid a key in a padlock, but before removing it, he pulled a gun from a pocket of the police pants he had bought in Beaune. He cocked the trigger, holding it steady as he lifted the padlock and opened the door. Henderson was collapsed on the floor, the loaf of bread gone, two empty bottles of water lying next to him. There was a pool of vomit on the other side. "Dear me, brother. Rough night?" Cobra laughed as he pulled another loaf of bread and two more waters from his bag and set them on the ground. "Another gourmet meal, brother."

He backed out of the dungeon, never taking his eyes from the man passed out on the floor. Martin wasn't above faking unconsciousness so he could catch his captor unaware. But the poor man didn't move. If it wasn't for the faint rise and fall of his chest, Cobra would swear that he was dead. He closed the door behind him and refastened the lock. He stood there, listening for the pathetic man to scurry for the food...*like the rats in the cave beneath Paris.*

He waited; it was quiet...nothing but the breeze echoing through the tall grass. Then he heard it...breaths inside the cell, and the sound of something – *someone* – dragging across the floor. He imagined Henderson pulling his weak body to the bread and he smiled. *Eat, drink, and be merry, dear brother, for tomorrow you may die.*

CHAPTER 13

Place Bellecour, Lyon, France

Walter ran his hand through his hair as he walked among the shops and statues of Place Bellecour. He had reached Lyon hours ago, had taken a cab to the square, and had been walking around ever since. He was looking for Matt, or at least a clue to suggest that he had been there. He had hoped to maybe help him escape before Cobra even knew Walter was there. But so far, he had seen no sign of Matt or his kidnapper.

Being in Lyon was difficult, and not only because he was looking for his abducted nephew. His good friend, Sean MacPherson, Caretaker of the Morning Star organization, had lived outside Lyon for the past eight years; his wife lived there still. They had moved there so Sean could keep watch over the warship; the same ship that had been stolen just hours ago. Sean had been killed in the attack. Being so close to Sean's home only accentuated the horror of all that had happened. Maybe, if there was time, Walter would travel to his home to pay his respects to Sean's wife, Colleen.

The only good thing to come of the attack was that the man behind it, Dolf Mueller, had been killed, as well. His death had been confirmed by a soldier at the scene, who had told Walter that the man's body had been decimated by the blast. *"All that's left of him is his jacket."* Walter had asked the soldier to bring the jacket to him after his noon lecture in Paris so he could verify – and prove, if necessary – that it was, in fact, Germany's Vice-chancellor who had carried out the odious act. He was also hoping the jacket might hold a clue as to where Mueller had hidden the warship.

The only problem was that Walter wouldn't be in Paris after his lecture; he wasn't giving the lecture. So, on his way to Lyon, he had called the soldier and had asked him to hold onto the jacket until Walter got back to Paris. When might that be? He sighed as he looked around the square. *God only knows.*

It was late afternoon, and the sun had begun to fade in the western sky. He found a chair outside a café, set his briefcase beside him, and closed his eyes, turning his face to the sky. After a few minutes, a cloud passed over the sun, and a burst of cold air forced him to zip his jacket. He scanned the square, again lamenting Cobra's choice of Lyon. Not only for the sadness it evoked as a result of Sean's death, but because of a specific memory that Walter shared with the son who was causing so much trouble. Had Mark – Cobra – chosen the square out of some sick sense of justice for all that had happened...*in the place where it first began?*

He breathed in, scents of coffee and cassoulet taking him back to that time, the only time he had come to Place Bellecour. It hadn't been for pleasure. The infamous Nazi, Klaus Barbie, *the Butcher of Lyon,* had been jailed in nearby Prison St. Paul, and Walter had been called on to aid in the man's defense. Why? Because Barbie had been vital in helping Walter undercut the Soviets' hold over Latvia.

The trial had begun in May of 1987, and had lasted most of the summer. Walter had known Barbie as Klaus Altmann, a counter-intelligence agent working for the United States, whose efforts to fight the communist influence in East Germany had contributed to the country's eventual liberation. Walter, who at the time had been working to help the Latvians break free of Russia, had met with the man many times, and had known him only as a friend to the West.

Walter tried to keep a low profile internationally, and had asked that his ties to the trial be kept out of the news. For the most part, the request had been honored, especially by

Barbie's lawyer, Jacques Verges. The man desperately needed Walter's testimony. Verges had called on Walter, along with investor Francois Genoud, to attest to Barbie's contributions in the fight against Communism. But the more Walter learned of Barbie's holocaust crimes, the more he had hated what he was being asked to do. Barbie had carried out some of the most despicable crimes of the holocaust, most of them in that very city. Just thinking of it now made him grimace. *How could I have vouched for such a man?* The simple answer: he had had no choice.

But he had tried to take advantage of the time away, and had decided to bring his insolent son with him. Mark had just turned twelve, and was already showing his defiance. Walter and Nenita had decided that a trip away – alone with his father – might calm the angry boy. Though the trial would last for weeks, Walter's role would take only a few days, and he had looked forward to spending time with his troubled son. But the trip had been a disaster; Mark had acted out every chance he got, going so far as to vandalize a statue of Louis the XIV, writing obscenities across its stone base. The minute Walter's role in the trial had ended, he had flown Mark home. On the way, he had made arrangements for the boy's admission into a boarding school outside Baclayon. The school had seemed perfect at the time. Strict, structured, intolerant of bad behavior, Walter had thought that the boy would be well-controlled, and eventually renewed. It was only later that he learned what had gone on at the school; the actions that had made his son not a better man, but a killer. Mark had reacted to his environment like any troubled boy might...with hatred and spite, which soon turned to rage and insanity. *And this square was where it all began.*

He shifted anxiously as he looked around...remembering. In spite of Mark's behavior, there had been moments of joy. Strolls among the shops in search of rare coins; the delight in Mark's eyes when he found one that he had never read about. A hop over bushes or a dash in the park as he laughed at things other children laughed at. And climbs in the hills outside Lyon when he would run ahead and say, *"Hurry, Father, come catch me!"* But then, suddenly, he would change. His disparate eyes would grow dark, and he would become the boy Walter now knew; he would become a monster. Walter would watch in stunned silence, knowing he was poorly equipped to handle whatever it was that had taken over the boy. He had blamed himself, though he didn't know why, and had spent the last seventeen years of his life trying to either fix it or make amends. He shook his head and sighed. He had failed miserably.

But it had taken him years to understand the ramifications of what Mark had become. He had eventually placed him in an asylum, but even after the boy – who by then was a man – had escaped amid a fire that he had likely started, Walter had been reluctant to do more than watch as his son terrorized the locals, breathing a sigh of relief when he finally left town. It was only after the murder of a priest outside the Vatican, when the killer's face was pasted on the front page of every European newspaper, that he had been forced to face the truth: He and Nenita had given birth to a killer. Though he had spent years deluding himself as to who – and what – Mark really was, from that moment on, he had vowed to do all that he could to find him and stop him. The only thing he couldn't do was tell anyone of his tie to the man that the world now knew as Cobra; not the authorities...not even Dora, his wife of fifty years.

Which makes me guilty, as well. He rubbed the back of his neck and leaned against the chair, disgusted with the choices he had made. He looked up at the Prison St. Paul where Barbie had been housed during the trial, frowning as he noted its location so close to the lovely Basilica Fourviere. A menacing prison...a beautiful cathedral. *Like Barbie – like all of us – bad and good, side by side.*

"Walter! Walter Henderson!" He looked up, stunned that someone would recognize him there. It wasn't a man's voice...the hopeful sound of his nephew calling to him. No, it was the cry of a woman, and, as he looked to see who it was, he was surprised. Coming his way, guarded by two wary agents, was Cynthia Madison.

Maddi was shocked to see Walter Henderson sitting only three tables away. She had seen him about twelve hours earlier at the de Crillon Hotel, and was curious what might have compelled him to travel to Lyon. *Did Matt text him, as well?*

She was hesitant to approach him; she would have to explain her presence in the square. *Maybe it's time, Maddi...time for him to know the truth about his son.* She had hated carrying that burden alone. If anyone should know, it should be his father.

She yelled his name and he looked her way, clearly surprised that he had been recognized. She noted again how much he looked like Martin...as if she was looking at her lover in thirty years. Her heart ached as she dared to hope that she and Henderson would be together in thirty years...*or even in thirty minutes.* She walked up to him. "It's good to see you again so soon, Walter."

He stood and smiled. He was one of the most handsome older men she had ever seen. Though the years were evident in graying temples and lines in his forehead and by his eyes, those eyes were kind and youthful. *Martin's eyes.* "It's good to see you, too," he said, frowning as he added, "I wonder if it's for the same reason."

Maddi's heart skipped a beat. "Matt texted you?"

"Not exactly. His cousin did."

Maddi was confused. *Matt's cousin is Martin...who is actually Matt. Walter doesn't know Martin's alive...does he?* She sighed. *There's only one way to find out.* "Walter, there's something I need to ask you." She pulled a chair next to him. They sat down. She nodded at her agents; they took a step back to give her privacy.

"What is it, Senator?"

"First, I'd like it if you would call me Maddi. That's how my good friends refer to me." She leaned closer and whispered "Are you aware of who Matt really is?"

Walter frowned, then shook his head and said angrily, "I knew it."

"Knew what?"

"That he wasn't who he said."

Maddi was confused. "What did he say?"

"That he was my nephew, who had supposedly died when he was two...but that he hadn't died after all." He sighed. "So, tell me...who is he really?"

Maddi held her breath. *He doesn't know!* She exhaled. *Should I tell him?* "Walter, how much do you know about the fire that...killed...your son?"

Walter flinched. "Why are you asking?"

"Bear with me, please. How much do you know?"

Walter tightened his jaw. "I know that a desperate man blew up a hotel, along with himself," his voice broke, "...and that Martin was...killed in the fire."

Maddi's heart was breaking. She leaned even closer and put her hand on his forearm. "Walter," she whispered, "...Martin...didn't die."

Walter pulled back. Maddi tried to imagine what he was feeling. Heartbreak? Relief? Anger that he hadn't known? *Likely all three.* She went on. "He was terribly scarred, so he had surgery...lots of surgeries, actually. He looks quite a bit different."

Walter's blue eyes grew pale as he stared at her. She could see the anguish in those eyes; the desire to believe her, with a caution that he shouldn't. She tightened her grip on his forearm. "I...I just found out...for certain...two days ago."

Maddi could feel Walter shaking. He said nothing; he didn't need to. She saw the hint of a smile, but it was short-lived as he digested what he had just been told. His son had survived, but hadn't told his own father he was alive...for four years. She got it; she had known that same feeling, that same anger, that same question of why.

A tower rang out a single chime. Maddi kept her hand on his arm, her eyes fixed on the eyes that were so like Martin's. Without looking away, and with a far different voice...a terrified voice, he said, "So, Cobra's holding *Martin*, not Matt?"

Maddi frowned. "No...no, Martin escaped. Isn't that what your text said?"

Walter put his hand over hers. She could barely hear him as he said, "No, Maddi, my text was from Cobra. He most definitely still has Matt...or Martin...and I'm certain that he plans on killing him."

Ah, my prey has made it easy for me. Cobra stared through the binoculars, the stone ledge he was standing on giving him a perfect vantage point. He had made it from the dungeon to the square in twenty minutes, and, though he looked the part of a captain in the *Gendarmerie nationale* – the French military police – he stayed out of sight behind the branches of a thick Fraser Fir. He couldn't risk Madison or Walter spotting him...*not yet.* He wore a light blue jacket with proper insignia, and had on the classic puckered pants with high boots. Not exact, but close. He snickered as passersby looked at him with respect, and a bit of fear. *Like the priest...with a gun.*

He kept his eye on Walter, impressed that he had responded so quickly to the text. Cobra had sent it around eight that morning – less than nine hours ago – and Boston was at least seven or eight hours from Lyon. *Daddy must've put the pedal to the metal in that leer jet of his.* Or, could it be that he had already been in France? In Paris for the NATO conferences, perhaps? If so, where was Dora? Wouldn't she have come with him? Cobra spat at the trees. *No...she probably hates him as much as I do.*

He looked from Walter to Madison and grinned. Soon they would see their cherished Martin lying on the floor of a dingy prison cell. Was Walter aware that Martin had survived the hotel blast four years ago? Jacob had said that no one else knew "...except for me, his girlfriend bitch...and now you." Cobra watched as Madison put her hand on Walter's arm. *Is she telling him now?* He gripped the binoculars, hoping to see the man's pain as he learned that he had been deceived. Cobra grinned. Was that anger he saw as Walter's eyes narrowed and the lines on his forehead deepened? Or was it sadness? The one emotion he saw no sign of was joy. Wouldn't he delight at the news? *Not when he's been lied to for the past four years.*

Cobra slid the binoculars in his pocket and jumped from his perch. He put on his sunglasses, and paraded up and down in front of the statue of Louis XIV. He stopped, suddenly kneeling at the stone base, half-expecting to see – seventeen years later – the swearwords that young Mark Villamor had written so many years ago. They were gone, and he grinned as he thought of those who had been forced to scrape them away. *Neither Mark, nor I, will be scraped away so easily this time.*

He stood and leaned against the statue. He took off his cap and shook out his long hair, combing his fingers through it as he stared up at the sun. He adjusted his sunglasses, which hid his oddly-colored eyes. He had been unable to bear the thought of wearing the scratchy blue contact lenses...*at least not yet*. Fortunately, it was a sunny day and no one would think twice about an officer wearing a pair of Oakley's.

He put on the hat, stuffing his hair underneath as he walked back to his ledge. He climbed to his spot behind the fir and glanced at his watch. *Four-fifty.* He looked at the serene Place Bellecour and smiled as he saw a mother pushing a stroller near where Madison and Walter were sitting. There were two old men playing chess to their other side, and a group of school children were following a teacher to the statue. One of them bumped Walter's elbow; Walter grinned at the boy with warmth. Cobra felt his stomach cramp. He turned his gaze on a young man darting past on a scooter. The teacher yelled, "Ralentir!" *Slow down!* Cobra sneered. *Such a tranquil scene.*

He took off the sunglasses and looked through the binoculars, scanning the square. There were no police in sight. He had learned that many of the local officers had been called to Paris to help with security for the NATO conference. He chuckled. *They're probably afraid that I might show up.*

He continued to scan the square, stopping when he got to Madison's agent, Spencer Seacroft, the man he had come to know so well. He watched him; the way he stood, the way he hovered over Madison so faithfully. Tall, lean, and physically capable, the agent was never more than a foot or two away from the senator. Cobra had hacked into the Secret Service data base and had read Seacroft's biography, as well as his prior assignments. Why? So he would have a tool to use against the man.

And what a tool I found, he thought with a grin. Seacroft's story was a profile of agonizing grief, from which had sprung a devotion to service. He lived with his grandmother outside DC; she was his only living relative. His parents had been killed right in front of him when he was only fourteen years old. It was clear from his biography that their violent death had taken a toll on him, and had eventually led him to his current vocation. Cobra straightened. *Of course, it did. The loss of a parent – be it through death or mere negligence – always takes a toll.*

He stayed focused on the agent. Yes, Cobra knew about Seacroft; he had made a point of knowing about him the minute he had decided to kidnap the senator. He even felt a bit of kinship with the man. Like Cobra, Seacroft's loss of his parents had defined him. Cobra scoffed. *What does he know? He had his parents for fourteen years. I lost mine the second I was born.*

Details regarding the murder of Seacroft's parents were tragic. They had been gunned down by an irate former employee in a shopping mall outside DC. Seacroft had been there, and he had suffered. As a result, he was weak. *He is vulnerable.*

Cobra scanned the faces in the square, trying to spot the three men he had hired just minutes ago. It had been easy to spot outcasts...those with nothing to lose. He had offered them a hundred euros apiece. *"All you have to do is stir up a bit of chaos."* They had been so willing. Three young men, important to no one, ready to do whatever he asked for a little bit of cash.

He grinned; he spotted one of them walking toward the center of the square. Cobra didn't know his name; it didn't matter. He called him "Mr. Big." He was about six-six with huge arms and an ample gut; an intimidating force, to say the least. Cobra had given him a pistol and a bag of C4 explosives. Mr. Big would get things started.

Where are your friends, big boy? Cobra's eyes lit up; he spotted them walking in from the opposite corner. They were smaller; wiry, dirty, with scars on their hands and faces from street fights that had gone bad. One wore a red beret; Cobra had christened him "Red." The other wore a gold chain; he was "Goldie." They, too, had been given pistols and C4, and he watched with glee as they strutted to the center of the square, eager to enact their rage on a crowd of innocents.

He looked at the tower clock: 4:58. *"Karma kills at five!"* Those were the words the man at the DC mall had said before he had annihilated Seacroft's parents and anyone else standing within ten feet of the store from which he had been fired. *And they are the words that will be said now.* Cobra had discovered that little detail in the crime scene transcript. The former employee had apparently been let go at five p.m. the day before, and had screamed those words while playing a song over the mall's PA system as his shooting spree began. Seacroft would know those facts; the music, the odd words screamed out so loudly. Why? *Because he was there.*

Cobra watched as Mr. Big walked to the center of the square. Red and Goldie had stopped only yards away and they both had their hands in their pockets, ready to set loose the fireworks. Cobra chuckled; those young men were about to die, and they didn't even care. *They died a long time ago.*

"Now, where are Seacroft's 'mom and dad'?" Cobra muttered as he scanned Place Bellecour. He spotted a couple walking in from the southwest corner and nodded. "There they are." He watched as they guided one another through the busy square. *Okay, Seacroft, here's the part you won't be able to resist.* He had spotted the couple on the patio behind the basilica as he was on his way back from the dungeon. Similar to Seacroft's parents, they looked to be in their early fifties, and the man shuffled as he walked, just like Seacroft's veteran father might have done. The woman held his arm tenderly, keeping him steady. They were dressed as Seacroft's parents might have dressed; the woman even had the same hair color as Seacroft's mother. Cobra couldn't have found a better match if he had had months to search.

The minute he had spotted them, he had run down the stairs and into a café, demanding a sheet of paper from a man behind a bar. He had quickly drawn up an official-looking document, then had rolled and tied it with a ribbon from his uniform. He had walked it over to the couple, and, presenting it on behalf of the *Gendarmerie,* had told them that they had won a sweepstakes, and would receive their prize at five o'clock in the center of the square. He chuckled. *And what a prize it will be!*

He continued to watch them. Suddenly, he saw the woman turn and speak to a younger lady. *A daughter?* He hadn't noticed her earlier. He bristled and lowered the binoculars. Seacroft was an only child. Would it matter? He sneered. *I won't let it.*

Everything was in place. Cobra stared at the tower clock, waiting, watching as the larger hand finally hit the twelve. The chimes for five o'clock began. He pulled a remote from his pocket and pushed a button. From somewhere in the trees on the other side of the courtyard, Queen's "Bohemian Rhapsody" filled the air. The three hired men went into action. Mr. Big, who had been standing near a café, suddenly yelled in English, "Karma kills at five!" The music continued. Mr. Big yelled it again. When the music had reached the part where Freddie Mercury sings, *"Mama, I just killed a man,"* Mr. Big fired a shot in the air. He yelled again, "Karma kills at five!" The man on the scooter sped by in an effort to get out of the way. Mr. Big shot him, killing him instantly with a bullet to the head. The music kept blaring. Red and Goldie ignited their C4 in the middle of the square. Place Bellecour erupted in fireworks. Cobra trained his binoculars on Seacroft. The man had pulled out his gun, had toppled a table, and had shoved Madison behind it. He was scanning the square. Had he heard the cry? Mr. Big yelled again, "Karma kills at five!" Cobra searched Seacroft's face, tightening the lens so he could read every twitch, every spasm. The agent turned and spoke to the second agent. They aimed their guns and fired. Mr. Big, who was holding a handful of lit C4, fell to the ground, bullets hitting his forehead and chest. The C4 exploded, igniting the square even more as screams of terror mixed with the music and the flares, creating a cacophony of utter chaos. *How wonderful!*

Cobra looked for the older couple. He spotted the daughter hurrying them to a kiosk at one end of the square. He laughed aloud as he saw the man clinging desperately to his wife. Had Seacroft seen them? Again, Cobra trained his binoculars on Seacroft. He magnified the lens, eager to watch the man react to the trap that had been laid out so perfectly. The music continued. *"I sometimes wish I'd never been born at all..."* Now it was Goldie's turn. He waited for a break in the lyrics, then yelled "Karma kills at five!" His voice was louder, and, in spite of the fireworks, it rang out across the square. Seacroft, who had been saying something to Madison, must have finally heard it, as he stopped and stared at Goldie. He scanned the square and, right on script, his eyes widened and his jaw dropped. He had spotted the couple. *How utterly delightful!* Cobra looked for Red and Goldie. They had been instructed to kill the couple *"...once the explosions begin."* The two men were skulking between tables, inching closer to the kiosk. They stopped and raised their guns. Cobra looked from them to Seacroft, grinning as he saw Seacroft turn and yell something to the second agent, who shook his head and yelled something back. Seacroft seemed to ignore him. Cobra was ecstatic. *Yes! The fool is going to try to save them.* Cobra raised his weapon and found Seacroft in his sight, just waiting for the right moment.

"Karma kills at five!"

Seacroft shook his head in disbelief. Had he heard it right? The cry was repeated. He felt unsteady and grabbed the table. It was bad enough when "Bohemian Rhapsody" had begun to play, but once he heard the yell from the courtyard, he was at a loss to stay focused. He forced his attention back to his protectee, but couldn't get the song or the shouted words out of his mind. He knew that song and those words; he had heard them before. He *felt* them. That mix of music and strange words yelled by a killer had repeated a thousand times in his mind. *"Karma kills at five."*

He saw Maddi trying to look over the edge of the toppled table. "Stay down, Maddi!" he yelled as he turned back to the square. He spotted an older couple huddled next to a kiosk. Clearly frightened, they were doing their best to hide from the mayhem. As he watched them, they seemed to change before his eyes. They were no longer strangers; a man with a cane, a woman by his side. No, they had become parents...*his parents...his mom and dad.* He shook his head, blinked, and looked again. *Oh my god, they're here!* It was impossible, but it was true. They were there...in Place Bellecour. And he was finally getting the chance to save them.

"I'm going out there, Brooks! Cover me!"

"Have you gone mad? It's total chaos!"

"I'm going! I have something I need to do...now cover me!"

He leapt into the square, doing his best to dodge bullets and steer clear of the C4. He kept his eyes on the couple. "I'm coming, Mom and Dad!" He sprinted toward them and was about to dive at them to protect them from stray bullets, when he felt a sharp pain in the side of his neck. He fell to the ground and slapped his hand over his neck. He felt blood...a lot of it. His carotid artery had been hit. He put pressure on it as he searched the square for his parents. His vision began to blur and he could barely hear. The music was the only thing registering. *"If I'm not back again this time tomorrow...carry on, carry on..."* He gasped for air and looked up at the sky, blinded by a combination of blood and tears. "God, forgive me...I have failed them again."

From her vantage point looking over the edge of the table, Maddi had watched in horror as her agent had run into the firefight. She had yelled for him to stop, but he had ignored her. She was stunned to see him leap in the air, his arms seeming to reach for an older couple who were huddled near a kiosk. She was even more stunned to hear him cry out to them as if he knew them. She looked on in horror as he fell to the ground and slapped his hand over his bloodied neck.

She lunged from behind the table and was taking a step toward him, when a strong hand pulled her back behind the table and shoved her to the ground. It was Brooks. She glared at him ready to fight him off but stopped when she saw his face; it was as white as a sheet. He yelled, "No senator, stay put! There's nothing we can do."

Cobra shoved his pistol in his pocket and trained his binoculars on the second agent, laughing when he saw him yank Madison to the ground. He was using one arm to restrain her, the other to aim at the two men who had shot the couple by the kiosk. The agent pulled the trigger: once, twice, three times. Cobra watched as first Red, then Goldie, fell to the ground. The C4 in their pockets ignited from nearby flames, and soon the entire square was on fire. The music was blaring, *"I see a little silhouetto of a man..."* People were running in all directions trying to escape not only the shooters, but the explosions. Cobra clapped his hands. *Utterly fantastic!*

He looked for Walter. He spotted him crawling behind a tipped table to get to Madison. *Perfect.* He tossed the binoculars into the trees, put on his sunglasses, and jumped from the ledge, falling easily into his role as a French policeman. "Everyone, stay calm!" he yelled in French. But no one noticed him. He pulled out his gun and, holding it in the air, shoved his way through the crowd. He edged closer to Walter, Madison, and her agent. The agent had managed to keep Madison behind the table, while at the same time keeping his gun aimed at the square. Cobra had read about that agent, as well. Nigel Brooks was a member of Her Majesty's Service, and was one of the finest sharp-shooters in the brigade. *I will have to kill him from behind.*

Sirens could be heard in the distance, their high-pitched warnings a crescendo to the symphony playing out in the square. Suddenly Cobra stopped, overcome by the moment. He removed his glasses, scanned the square, and smiled. The smile became a laugh as he raised his gun, and, using it as a baton, kept time with the music, pulling in imaginary trumpets and snares as if conducting his very own symphony. Unlike anything he had ever felt, the sense of power and perfection was intoxicating.

He heard more sirens. *Get moving, Cobra!* He put on his glasses and resumed his role as a French policeman. He slid through the crowd, closing the gap as he watched Walter and the agent form a shield around Madison. He wielded his gun with authority, blending in with the frightened citizens as he shouted unnoticed orders in French. He edged closer, finally getting to within ten feet of his targets. The Rhapsody continued, *"Easy come, easy go, will you let me go...."*

He was about to shoot the agent when he felt a tug on his sleeve. He turned to see the same woman he had seen with the couple in the square; the woman he guessed was their daughter. She was pulling at his jacket, tears streaming from her eyes. In French she cried, "Help me, officer! My parents...have been shot!"

Shut up, you bitch! He ignored her, again focusing his gun on the agent.

"Please officer!" the young girl pleaded, hysterical as she pulled on his sleeve.

He sighed, reached behind him, and smacked her across the jaw. She fell to the ground, stunned. He laughed. "Get used to it, Sweetie. Life's full of betrayal."

He then turned to his prey, aimed his gun, and shot the agent in the back of the head.

Walter saw Brooks fall to the ground, and immediately grabbed the agent's gun. He crawled to a point that would put him between Maddi and where the shot had come from. He couldn't see a shooter; all he saw was a policeman running toward him. His heart was racing, his hands shaking as he looked for the man who had fired the shot. He saw a woman on the ground with her lip bleeding, and a young man with two small children running for the trees, but no shooter. He yelled at the officer, "Did you see who fired that shot?"

The policeman removed his glasses, and Walter's stomach turned. The man – his mismatched eyes unmistakable – laughed as he said, "Why, hello Daddy."

Maddi stared at Brooks lying on the ground beside her. She reached for his hand; it was cold. She saw the blood oozing from the back of his head. There was no doubt in her mind; the wound was fatal. She edged closer and looked in his eyes.

111

The life was fading from them. She tried to comfort him and assess the wound, while fighting an overwhelming sense of panic. Both of her agents had been shot and were either dead or dying. She was about to yell for Walter to help with Brooks, when she saw him raise the gun he had taken from the agent and aim it at a police officer. She gasped. *Why is Walter about to shoot a cop?*

Walter was shaking. *It can't be!* But there was no mistaking those eyes. He was staring at his son; his *other* son...*the one who is a mass murderer.* He didn't hesitate as he put his finger on the trigger and fired. But before the bullet could leave the chamber, he felt a sharp pain in his shoulder as Cobra was able to get off a shot, then leap out of the way. Walter's shot missed Cobra, hitting a tree instead. Walter's gun fell to the ground and he grabbed his shoulder. "You son of a bitch!"

"An interesting choice of words, Daddy." The sirens were getting closer, and there were more of them. Cobra aimed his gun at Walter. "You and the senator, come with me...now! I have to get you *criminals* to jail...so you can join my dear brother."

Walter stared at Cobra. What Maddi had told him was true. He barely noticed the gun or the man holding it, as he thought with a mixture of grief and joy...*Dear God...my son is...alive!*

Seacroft's anger at his shooter was surpassed only by his anger at himself. He could feel the blood draining from him; his only wish was that it would happen fast. He had failed his parents. He had failed Maddi. He didn't want to live. He forced his eyes open; the light from the fire in the square was overwhelming. He saw a statue not far away; he thought he saw the man on the horse give him a nod. *My greeting to the afterlife.* He could hear music, screams, gunshots, sirens; the sounds were distant, as if he was miles away. He looked for Maddi. He was encouraged when he saw a policeman walking toward her. All at once, the officer stopped, removed his sunglasses, and smiled as he scanned the square. Seacroft frowned. *How can he be smiling?* There was something wrong. Seacroft tried to get up. He couldn't.

His eyes closed and he faded away, soothed by an image of his mom and dad. No longer were they hiding behind a kiosk, or lying bloody and dead on the floor of a shopping mall outside DC. No, they were alive and well...he could hear them calling to him. He wanted to go, but something was holding him back; as if he was being pulled in different directions. "I'm coming," he said, as he felt strong arms lift him. The image of his parents began to fade. He heard someone yell, "Hurry, we're losing him!" and felt himself being hoisted into an ambulance. He felt a jolt to his chest, then another one. "He's back!" someone yelled. He heard doors slam and felt the van move. He was being saved. He wanted to scream, "No! Let me die!" but his voice wouldn't come. As the ambulance pulled away, all he could hear was the music in the square, "*...nothing really matters, anyone can see...nothing really matters to me.*"

Maddi covered her ears, the noise deafening as fire overtook the square. The roar of the flames, the blare of the sirens, the panic of the screams blended into a horrible discord and she felt like she was about to faint. She couldn't take her eyes off of Walter, who had just tried to shoot a cop. She jumped up when she saw blood spurting from his shoulder, and ran to check the wound. Her fingers shook as she probed where the bullet had entered. "It went on through, Walter, but...but you need a hospital!" She wrapped her red scarf like a tourniquet over the wound.

Walter shook his head, surprisingly calm. "There'll be no hospital, Maddi."

The music ended, but the sirens were getting louder. Maddi looked at Walter. "What are you taking about?" She turned to the officer, who was grinning. He had his gun aimed at Walter. She frowned. "Why are you smiling? This man needs a doctor!"

The policeman chuckled. "Why don't you explain things, Walter."

Walter kept his eye on the officer. Calmly, in a voice that defied the moment, he said "I'm fine, Maddi. And this...*officer*...won't hurt us, not yet, anyway." He turned to Maddi. She was surprised to see that his eyes were filled with rage. "This man is the Cobra, Maddi, and he won't do anything to us...until Martin can watch."

Maddi stared at Walter, then at Cobra, too stunned to speak. She knew of the Cobra; he was the man responsible for the murder of the Secretary of State at the Queen's Ball. But why did he care about Walter, or Henderson...*or me?*

She saw a police car at the other end of the square. Two officers were shoving through the crowd. Cobra must have seen them, too, as he snapped, "Let's go!"

Maddi looked down at Brooks, her heart breaking. "We can't just leave him."

Cobra cocked the trigger of his gun and held it to Walter's head. "Yes, we can. Now move or I blow out his brains."

Maddi's entire body was shaking. She grabbed Walter's arm, closed her eyes, and stepped over the dying Brooks. Cobra directed them to a group of rocks at the far end of the square. Hidden behind shop awnings amid late-afternoon shadows, the rocks were invisible to anyone in the square. Cobra shoved them toward one of the rocks and snapped, "Climb." Neither one moved. "Climb!" he yelled, and held the gun to Walter's head.

Walter went first, scaling the rock easily. He then helped Maddi, while Cobra climbed the rock next to them. When they had reached the other side, Cobra forced them up a rise through thick brambles to a field of tall grass behind the basilica.

"Keep moving!"

When they were a safe distance from the square, Cobra ordered them to throw their phones to the ground. "If I find either one of you is hiding a weapon or a phone, I'll shoot both of you *and* your beloved Martin; got it?"

Maddi looked at Walter. He nodded, "It's okay," then threw down his phone. Maddi did the same. Cobra put a bullet through each and shoved Maddi. "Let's go."

She led the way; Walter followed. She couldn't stop shaking. Seacroft and Brooks had been shot, and she and Walter were being taken to who knew where. *Hopefully, to Henderson...who is hopefully still alive.*

She thought of Seacroft and had to stifle a cry. He was more than an agent; he was her friend. She prayed the bullet hadn't found its mark, but, as she thought of him lying on the ground with blood pouring from his neck, she knew that it had.

And dear Nigel. He had been sucked into this drama unwittingly, and now he, too, was lying dead in the square. She felt sick. This was what happened to any man who got close to her. *Stop it, Maddi...you didn't kill them, Cobra did.*

She tripped and fell to her knees. She trembled as she felt the cold steel of a pistol nudge her temple. "Get up, bitch. Your lover's waiting."

CHAPTER 14

Washington, DC

"A good plan, violently executed now, is better than a perfect plan next week." Morningstar chuckled as he thought of the General Patton quote. It was fitting. Though everything was moving more quickly than he had intended, it was moving nonetheless, and Conner had been its first victim. The man had been easier to manipulate than a mutt in Pavlov's lab. *Conner, you're a fool.* It was as if he had been following a script, and Morningstar had been astounded at how quickly the VP had folded. *It didn't hurt that ole Betsy was on board.*

He stood from his desk in his corner office on the first floor of the Pentagon and walked to the only window. It looked out on a courtyard, and Morningstar often gauged his mood on the weather outside. Today, it was cold and rainy, with hefty gusts of wind. He chuckled. *A picture-perfect day to start the takeover of the world.*

He had had that corner office for quite some time now, having secured the spot through his loyalty to the Chairman of the Joint Chiefs, Alexander Daniels. He had served the man faithfully for the past twenty-five years, and had every intention of staying in his service for as long as Daniels was at the Pentagon. Why? Because Daniels – and Morningstar's role as his aide – gave Morningstar power...a power available to very few men. He smiled as he watched the wind blow the barren trees as if they were twigs. *Not only that; the man would be nothing without me.*

His cellphone vibrated; he answered with a quick "Yes."

"Father, it's me."

Morningstar's heart warmed at the sound of Judah's voice. "What is it, son?"

There was a pause. "Um...the damnedest thing just happened." Another pause. "I...I just received a call from...Wilcox." A pause. "He asked me if I wanted..." Judah's voice dropped to a whisper, "...to be...his VP."

Morningstar grinned at Knight's childlike naivete. What had he thought would happen once Morningstar forced Conner out of the job? "What did you tell him?"

"Why, I said yes, of course." A pause. "It's what I was supposed to do, right?"

Morningstar chuckled. "Yes, it's exactly what you were supposed to do."

"Why do you suppose...the VP...chose to leave now? I mean the election's less than eight months away."

Morningstar had to fight not to laugh. "It's hard to say, Judah. Maybe the rigors of the job were just too much for him."

"Perhaps." A pause. "I wonder why Wilcox chose me?"

"You're well-qualified, Judah. A true asset, from where I sit."

Another pause. "I guess so. Anyway, I just wanted you to know, sir."

"Certainly, son. I'll look forward to hearing more."

Morningstar ended the call. Things couldn't have gone better. Wilcox had wasted no time in calling Knight. Though the senator from Florida was the best candidate by far, it likely hadn't hurt that Morningstar had had his aide, Josh Adams, who was also a son of Jacob, sneak in a sheet of paper with polling data showing Knight's high favorability ratings and lay it on the President's desk earlier in the day.

He slid the phone in his pocket and grinned. Yes, things were coming along nicely. Regardless of what happened next,

Morningstar would soon have one of his sons within a few yards of the Oval Office.

And he couldn't have picked a more capable candidate than Jerome Knight. Raised by his own hand, tutored under the watchful eye of a surrogate senator, and trained by Morningstar's own personal army, Judah had been well-groomed for the role he was about to play. Though the timeline had been rushed, things were moving along exactly as planned. *That's what comes from wise and careful preparation.*

Jerome had been with him the longest of any of the sons, coming to him at the age of ten, long before God had fated Morningstar to be a modern-day Jacob. But, as if the prophecy had already taken hold, Morningstar had seen an opportunity and had taken it. Knight's father had been a respected 9th circuit judge, his mother was the daughter of a famous governor from Maine. They had only one child, ten-year-old Jerome, and no living relatives. The situation was irresistible. Morningstar, having been introduced to the family as a result of a Pentagon briefing regarding another 9th circuit judge, had seen his opportunity. It had begun with a tragic car crash that had resulted in the deaths of Jerome's parents. Morningstar had interceded, claiming to be a close family friend. There had been no one to challenge it, and he had immediately had Josh draw up formal documents that placed all the Knight's vast wealth in a trust, with Morningstar as trustee. A high-end lawyer on Morningstar's payroll had aided in the transfers. Once the trust was in place, Morningstar had taken it upon himself to place the boy, Jerome, with a cousin of the boy's mother, Senator Charles Sturgill from Maine. *"Raise him, Sturgill, and ready him for the world stage."* In exchange, Sturgill was promised insider help on his upcoming election, along with a lot of cash.

But there had been one more pledge given to Sturgill in exchange for his help. Morningstar had agreed to assist with the hunt for Sturgill's actual son, who had been taken years ago while the family was on a mission trip in China. Though Morningstar suspected that the child was dead, he had gone along with the request, using the Sturgill's own grief to entice them to raise the wealthy Jerome Knight as their own.

He grinned as he recalled Charles taking the boy from him that first night after the accident. The senator had looked at Morningstar and had said, *"I raise this kid, and you swear you'll help me find my boy?"* Morningstar had nodded. The man had added with no apparent shame, *"and you'll get me reelected, and give me lots of money...is that right?"* Morningstar had smiled. *"Yes, Senator, more money than you could ever imagine."* That had been the end of it. The Sturgill's had raised Jerome, and they had raised him well. In return, Morningstar had made sure that Sturgill was reelected –four times now – and had paid him handsomely through the years. As for Sturgill's lost son, Morningstar had made cursory inquiries, and felt certain the boy was dead. He couldn't tell Sturgill that; he would lose his cooperation. But the man brought it up often, and Morningstar knew that one day he would be forced to deliver.

He was still at the window. He took a last look at the overcast day and smiled. Yes, God had known what he was doing when he put Morningstar in charge. Though things were moving more quickly than he had intended, it was okay. Because a good plan, violently executed now, was better than a perfect plan next week.

CHAPTER 15

Lyon, France

Where is he taking us? Maddi's despair over the loss of her agents was matched only by her fear of being without them. She glanced at Walter, who was showing little resistance as Cobra shoved them both through the tall grass. When they were nearing the far edge of the field, Cobra grabbed Walter by his injured arm and swung him around to face him. "So, where's Dora?"

"She...couldn't make it." Walter said, wincing as Cobra pushed his thumb into the wound.

Cobra nodded. "I see. You sure got here fast. Kissed the bitch and left, eh?"

"I was already...in France," he gritted his teeth, "...on business."

Cobra frowned. "Well, the party won't be complete without her, so you need to get her here."

Walter narrowed his eyes. "No. I won't."

Cobra grinned, and a fading ray of sunlight highlighted his eyes. It was the first time Maddi realized that they were different colors. It was unsettling; as if the DNA hadn't only missed on the individual, but on the irises, as well. He laughed and it made her feel sick. "Then I will kill Martin...five minutes from now."

Walter pulled away. "No, Mark! You need to stop this...now!"

Cobra pushed his thumb even deeper into the wound. "I don't need to stop anything. I can do whatever I want. Kind of like you, *Daddy*."

Maddi frowned. There it was again...a reference to Walter being Cobra's father. It was absurd. *So why does he keep saying it?* Again, Maddi tripped and again, she fell to her knees.

Cobra looked down at her. "You certainly are a clumsy thing." He leaned down and blew on her forehead. "Tired from your trek?"

Maddi looked away, fighting the urge to scream.

Walter bristled. "Leave her alone, Mark." He tried to pull away; Cobra held him even tighter. Walter grimaced. "Okay, I'll...I'll call Dora. But she's in America. It will take...at least a day...for her to get here."

Cobra laughed. "We both know that isn't so, now don't we, Pops. You have a private jet – a Citation X, if I'm not mistaken – and all you need to do is to have the thing gassed up, get your wife on board, and have one of your pilots fly her ass to Lyon." Cobra glanced at his watch. "It's five-thirty here in France, which means it's eleven-thirty back in Boston. Wheels up by noon, she could be here by one a.m....two at the latest." He grinned. "That's a perfect time to start the party, don't you think?"

Walter shook his head. "It's not that simple. I have to give her a reason to stop what she's doing and fly to Lyon." He paused. "We're not exactly close, you know."

Cobra laughed. "No, I don't suppose you are." He turned to Maddi. "After all, when you screw another woman and she has your child, well, it puts a bit of distance between a husband and wife."

Maddi hid her shock as she glared at Cobra. Forcing her voice to stay calm, she said, "Bringing Mrs. Henderson into this...mess...makes no sense. Kill us...fine. But that poor woman already buried her son...years ago. Can't you leave it at that?"

Cobra leaned down, his face so close to hers she could feel the heat from his breath. He smiled. "Ah, a feisty one. You'll be fun." He stuck out his tongue, wiggled it, and leaned even closer. He whispered, "It's so much better when they fight."

Maddi shoved him but he didn't budge. He laughed. "Look bitch, there'll be no party without Dora."

Holding a gun on the two of them, he pushed Walter to his knees next to Maddi and tossed him a phone. It hit his chest and fell into the grass. "Call her. Put it on speaker. And don't try anything clever, or I'll pull out Marty's eyes one at a time."

Walter said nothing as he dug through the weeds for the phone. He found it, hesitated, then dialed. After a few seconds, Maddi heard a soft "Hello?"

"Dor—Dora? It's...Walter." He closed his eyes. "Um...listen...dear, something's come up." He paused. "I need you...to join me in Lyon...right away."

"Lyon? What happened to Paris?"

A longer pause. "Things have changed."

"I see. Well, I don't think I can make it, Walter. I have obligations here."

With a sternness Maddi guessed wasn't normal for him, Walter said, "You have to come, Dora!" Softer, he added, "It's...it's about...Martin. He's...alive, okay?" He added, even quieter, "Please come, Dora."

There was silence. Then, "Even for you, Walter, that is a horrid thing to say. I don't know what game you're playing, but—"

"I'm not playing, Dora. I don't have details, but I know that it's true. Call Gerald, tell him to get the plane ready. Try to leave Montgomery Airport by noon."

"I'll do no such thing." There was a pause. "Martin is dead, Walter." Quieter, she added, "No one could have survived that fire." Another pause. "And he most certainly wouldn't have allowed us to think he was dead if he wasn't."

She sighed. "So, where do you suggest he's been for the last four years?"

Walter shook his head. "I don't know. I haven't seen him...yet." He looked up at Cobra, who was smiling from ear to ear. Walter added, "Just take my word for it...he's alive, okay?"

"Take your word for it?"

Walter flinched. "I have it on good authority that he is alive...alright?" He took a deep breath. "I'll know more by the time you arrive."

Silence. Then, "Will...will you be there to meet me?"

Walter looked up at Cobra, who shook his head. "No, but someone will. He'll have your name written on a piece of cardboard." He closed his eyes and sighed. "See you soon, Dora." The call ended. No 'goodbye, I love you.' Just a pushing of the button as Walter threw the phone at Cobra. "There. You satisfied?"

Cobra slid the phone in his pocket. "I will be once she's here. It's clear she doesn't trust you." He chuckled. "Such a shame. Let's hope she does as you ask."

Walter bristled. "I've done what you said...now, let me see my son!"

Cobra struck a pose. "Ah, but you're looking at him...right, Daddy?" He grabbed Walter by his wounded arm and pulled him to his feet. He used his other hand to grab Maddi and stand her up. He pushed them. "Get moving...both of you."

They continued through the tall grass, until they reached a path that circled a steep ravine. They moved single file – Walter in front, Maddi behind him, Cobra in back – past the canyon. They came to a hill; Cobra shoved them and this time it was Walter who tripped. Maddi held out her hand; he grabbed it. She looked back at Cobra. He was laughing. "Rough terrain, eh Pops?" At the bottom of the hill, they came to a creek. Walter hesitated and Cobra pushed him. "It's just water."

Cobra was about to shove Maddi in after him, when she held up her hand and said, "I'm going." She stepped into the ice-cold stream, her heels sinking into the dirt. She couldn't take off her shoes; they were her only protection from the rough stones lining the bottom. The creek was about three feet wide; she slogged through it, her heels catching with every step. She reached the other side and tugged one foot, then the other from the sludge. She was chilled from the water and the cold air, and pulled her jacket – Henderson's jacket – tighter around her. She stooped down, took off her shoes, and did her best to shake off the mud. As she put them back on, she turned to Cobra. "I'm sure you're aware that the U.S. military will be looking for us." She cleared her throat. "They've probably got a chopper on the way as we speak."

Cobra laughed. "It doesn't matter, sweetie...they won't get here in time to save your lovely little ass." He shoved her and waved his gun. "Now, get moving!"

They came to a forest and hiked single file through rows of ancient maples. The fading sunlight streamed through bare branches, sending slivers of light to guide them. They stumbled over sticks, tree roots, and vines, reaching the far end just as a far-off tower rang out six chimes. They emerged into another field of tall grass. The shadows had grown heavy and she could barely see. The air felt like ice against her skin. She shivered and pulled Henderson's jacket even tighter as she looked around. She saw a row of hills and was about to look away, when she spotted a shadow on the second hill. Was it a tree? *Or is that a building?* She gasped. "Oh my god."

Cobra laughed. "Yes, my dear. Feast your eyes on the Dungeon of the Basilica Fourviere. Delightful, isn't it?" He shook his head, amused. "Oh, those Catholics and their secrets." He added, "I've dubbed the site, 'Henderson's Holy Hell'."

Henderson was freezing. The heat from the sun was gone. He fought to open his eyes, aware that he had passed out again. Whatever drug Cobra had given him wasn't leaving his body; he seemed to be getting worse, not better. He heard the tower bells and counted...*four, five, six.* He had been out for nearly two hours.

Maddi! The last words he had heard had come from Cobra telling him Maddi was on her way. Was it true or had he imagined it? Two hours had passed; she wasn't there. Though he would give anything to see her, he prayed that he had imagined it.

He lifted his head, and immediately wished he hadn't. The pain in his temples was unbearable. He closed his eyes and let his head fall to the ground. He was trying to not lose consciousness...or hope. But it was too late; he had already lost both.

Again, he thought of Maddi. He would soon be leaving her forever, but at least now she could go on with her life. *She's better off without me.*

Suddenly, his eyes flew open. He had heard something. Footsteps...outside? He listened; there was nothing. *You just imagined it, Henderson.* He closed his eyes again, and, as the evening shadows lengthened on the walls and ceiling, he wept.

Maddi sprinted to the second hill. The grass slowed her down, and her water-soaked shoes were creating blisters on her feet. She ignored it all as she climbed the hill and spotted a lone, shed-like building sitting amid the tall grass. The shadows of late day cloaked it in menacing gray, and she had to fight a crushing sense of despair. She saw a barred window high up on one side of the building and ran to it. She took a deep breath and yelled up to the window, "Henderson, it's me...it's Maddi!"

There was no reply. She said it again, this time louder. Still nothing. Were they too late? Had Cobra brought them there just to show them Henderson's dead body? She yelled again, then banged her fists on the jagged stone as she fell to her knees. *We're too late.* Walter ran up and knelt beside her. He said nothing as he laid a hand on her shoulder. She looked up at him, her throat tightening as she said, "I think we're...too late."

All at once, she heard a weak, raspy voice echo through the window. "Ma—Maddi, is that you?"

"Yes! Oh, God, yes, I'm here!"

"You have to go. He's going to kill you. I love you, but you must go...now!"

Cobra ran up behind them. "Too late, again, dear brother. The party's about to begin."

CHAPTER 16

Lyon, France

Cobra had watched Madison outside the prison and it had made him want to puke. *That poor, lovesick bitch,* he thought. *And comforted by my daddy...how special.* He waited, then stepped closer and kicked Walter's leg. "Let's go."

He walked them around the dungeon to the door, waving his pistol. "I'll say this only once. If either one of you tries to be a hero, I will kill the other one, and your precious Martin instantly. Do you understand?" Neither one said a word. Cobra raised his voice. "I *said* do you understand?" They nodded. He unlatched the lock, removed it from the door, and stepped back. "Madison, you go in first."

She pulled open the door and ran inside. Cobra laughed at how easily – how foolishly – she had let herself be put in danger. *All for love,* he thought with a sneer. Walter walked in after her, far more hesitant. *My father knows what I'm capable of.*

Madison went immediately to Henderson who was lying on the ground. She knelt down and put her hand to his cheek. "My god, what's he done to you?"

"My god, what's he done to you?" Cobra parroted. "Ask what's been done to *me!*"

Henderson opened one eye and offered her a weak, but genuine smile.

She hugged him, her entire body shaking.

He mumbled, "You...you shouldn't have come. He'll kill you."

"I don't care," she whispered, though Cobra was able to hear every word. She sat back on her heels and looked at Henderson. Tears fell from her eyes as she moved closer, hugged him again, then kissed him and laid his head on her lap. She took off her jacket and laid it over him. Again, Cobra felt like he might puke.

He waited to see what Walter would do. The man stared at Martin, then walked slowly to where he was lying. He knelt beside him. His voice cracked as he said, "My god...Martin." He wiped his eyes, then touched a strand of Martin's coal black hair. "Is it...is it really you?"

Cobra burst out laughing. "Oh, dear god, Daddy...you really didn't know!" His mirth turned to anger as he saw Walter – *his father* – reach down and embrace his other son, the imposter who had soaked in all the goodness, all the love, while little Mark Villamor was forced to put up with seconds. Cobra hissed, the sound surprising him as he kicked Walter in his wounded shoulder. "Get away from him!"

Walter winced, but said nothing, still holding the man – his *real* son – making no effort to move away from him.

Cobra cocked the gun from behind Walter's back. "I said, get away."

Walter laid Henderson's head back down on Maddi's lap. He stood and, not taking his eyes from Cobra's, walked toward him. "Go ahead...kill me, Mark. I don't care. I regret every minute of your sorry life. The fact that I'm responsible for you is a burden I can no longer carry." His eyes softened, as he added, "But I will say this; I'm...I'm sorry for not being whatever it was that you needed."

Cobra stared at him, stunned by the admission. He trembled, tempted by the man's candor, drawn in by his sudden acknowledgement that he had failed his "other" son. He felt a sense of grief wash over him, then quickly shut it down. "Is...is that what you think? That some *failure* on your part is what made me who I am?"

He paced the cell. "You still don't get it, do you Daddy?" His chest was heavy; he was finding it hard to breathe. "You didn't make me...except for that brief moment when you *screwed* my mother." He stopped to stand directly in front of him. "Circumstance *made* me." His hand was shaking. "I *made* me."

Suddenly, he felt the urge to write a poem. It was something he did quite often, actually. "Why, Pops, I do believe I feel a rhyme coming on." With his gun still aimed at Walter's forehead, he struck an orator's stance and said dramatically,

> "Why do snakes come out at night?
> Cause they alone don't need the light
> To see what others cannot see,
> The endless shame that by degree
> Puts forth the makings of a knife
> To cut my heart and steal my life..."

He waved the gun in the air; he had more to say, but was having trouble getting air. He took a deep breath, the effort making him cough, as he finished,

> "...I thank my dad from whence it came.
> He gave me that, but not his name."

He stopped and looked at them. They had gone silent. He had stunned them. It wasn't the first time his gift for rhyme had astounded his foes. He thought back to the witty prose he had shared with his half-brother when he had coaxed him through Paris in search of the CIA agent. "Not bad, eh?"

He stepped back, wielding his pistol in the air. "Don't you worry, Pops...I am exactly who I want to be." He had to fight not to pull the trigger. He ran up, kicked him in the shin, then stepped back. Walter fell forward onto his hands. Cobra laughed. "Your shame of me is your problem." He posed theatrically. "I kinda like me."

Again, he paced the small cell, making sure to stay far enough away that they couldn't ambush him. As he walked, he talked. "You see, Walter. It isn't about you...it never was. I was born out of necessity...to protect a child. But I have become so much more. It has become my fate to rid the world of the arrogant elite," he glared, "...you know, people like you." He coughed again. "And I started with that spineless headmaster." He turned to Madison. "It was I who saved the boy, Mark, you know."

Not waiting for her reply, he walked to the back of the dungeon and leaned against the wall. With the gun still aimed at them, he eased to the ground, finding comfort in the coolness of the stone wall. He put a hand to his head; he could feel a headache coming on. "Stay...away!" he yelled, but the headache was getting worse, and he could feel himself slipping away. "No...I'm not leaving!" He laid his head against the wall to fight off the headache; it was no use. He blinked and was stunned to see two ghostlike images appear out of nowhere. He became irate when he saw that one of them was the same man who had visited him in Paris; the irritating Mark Justice. Dressed in a bone-colored suit, he was strutting about with an arrogance that irked Cobra to his core. He had met men like Justice, men who felt themselves to be above it all; who saw themselves as overseers to those who were less...less wealthy, less handsome, less educated. Cobra spat at the image; Justice merely laughed.

"You're weary, Cobra. Let me have a go of it."

"I will never let you have a go of it, Justice!"

But it was the other ghost that had unnerved him...the child, Mark Villamor. The twelve-year-old boy was sitting to Cobra's left, hugging his knees as he rocked back and forth in fear. Cobra scowled. "Get a hold of yourself, child!"

"Now Cobra...he's just a boy," said Justice, who had sat to Cobra's right.

Cobra sneered. "Get out of here, Justice!"

The image didn't move. Neither image moved. Cobra had begun to shake. The boy looked up with wide eyes; Cobra tightened his jaw. "Don't look at me!"

"Cobra, you're upset." Justice said.

Cobra swung around to face the man and yelled, "Damn right, I'm upset. I'm upset because of you! Now, go...get out of here, Justice, and take that boy with you!"

Cobra jumped up and stomped into the middle of the ten-foot room. His legs were unsteady, his vision blurred, but still he was able to hold the gun on his captives. He took a quick look over his shoulder, hoping the two ghosts had left; they hadn't and it made him furious. He put his arms in the air and screamed, "Get out of here...both of you!" He waited; they didn't move. He stumbled back to the wall. His voice was far weaker as he said, "Go...get out."

But still they stayed, as if they were tied to him...as if they were part of his skin, his teeth, his hair. He yelled, "You better go, cause I'm sure as hell not leaving!"

Suddenly, out of the corner of his eye, he saw the faint outline of his father walking toward him. What was that on his face? Concern? *No! I'll not allow that man to care for me!* What happened to the fear that had been there just minutes before? With great force of will, he aimed the gun directly at his father, pulled back the trigger, and said coldly, "Don't...come...near me."

The man stopped, but didn't back away. "Mark, let me help you."

Cobra winced. "Shut up!" He caught a glimpse of the woman, Madison. She, too, had started to rise. "Sit down, bitch!" She sat, but he could see that her fear was gone, as well. It had been replaced by curiosity. Had she seen Justice? Had she seen the boy? *You can't let her see them!* But how could he hide them?

He was suddenly distracted by the image of the boy, who had crept to a far corner and was crouching, his wide eyes looking up at a headmaster who would soon whack him with his cane. Cobra turned and yelled, "It is the last time that headmaster will beat you, child!" He tried to see the headmaster so he could hurt him – *kill* him – all over again, but the man wasn't there. Cobra frowned. *If he's gone, they should be gone, too.* But still they stayed; still they sat against the back wall of the dungeon.

"Let me help you," said the well-dressed Justice as he stood and reached out his hand, echoing the very words that Cobra's father had just said.

"If one more of you says he wants to help me...just stay away, Justice!"

The image smiled. *"Calm down, Cobra. Give me the reins. You need to rest."*

Cobra yelled at the top of his lungs, "I don't want your help, Justice!"

Then, as quickly as they had come, the images vanished, lost to the mist of the dungeon. Cobra blinked, glad they were gone, but shamed as he looked at the stunned faces of his prisoners. *How much did they see?* He cleared his throat as he tried to regain his composure. Waving the gun with authority, he yelled, "Walter, sit next to Martin." He aimed the pistol at Madison. "You too, bitch. He's gonna die soon."

Walter didn't move. "Mark, I know what you must be feeling."

Cobra bristled. "You...have...no idea...what I'm feeling!" He spat at the man. "But soon you'll know...soon you'll know exactly what a little boy felt as he was beaten and tortured while you screwed his mom, then flew back to your fancy mansion." Cobra lunged at him and Walter jumped back. Cobra laughed and glared his hatred like a spear at the man's chest. "Now, get over there with the others!"

Walter walked over to Martin and knelt beside him. Cobra forced an even tone as he said, "I don't know if you're aware, *Daddy*...but I hate you. I have always hated you." The words gave him strength. "With each breath I take and with every beat of my Henderson heart, I *despise* you!" He could see Walter tremble...was it anger? Or was it fear? He grinned. It was fear...and it was invigorating.

Cobra paced the cell, the headache easing as he regained the upper hand. After another minute he stopped, faced his prisoners, and waved his gun in the air. "I'm sorry to have to leave so soon...we were having such fun, but I need to prepare for the others." He edged sideways to the door, keeping his eyes and his gun trained on the prisoners. "Now, behave. I'll be back before you know it."

He stepped outside and locked the door. The sun had set, leaving the air cold and the night dark. He breathed in, glad to be out of the stale prison with so many imposters. Not only the ghosts of the boy and Justice, but the real live images of his father who had never been more than a sperm donor, and his half-brother who had literally stolen the life that Mark Villamor was supposed to have lived.

He ran from the jail, glancing over his shoulder, half-expecting to see a weak child or a well-clad investigator following close behind. "You're not part of me," he said, "...so leave me alone!" He doubted they would. Though it was only the second time that Justice had come to him, that pathetic boy had lurked in his mind for as long as he could remember. They *were* a part of him; every bit as much as his spleen or his liver. But he didn't want them; he didn't *need* them. "I'm done with you, you hear?"

He trudged down the hill and through the tall grass. He reached the trees, trying to put the ghosts out of his mind. But he could feel them; the two Mark's, Villamor and Justice, lurking within, trying to somehow displace him. Distant chimes rang out from the cathedral, and from somewhere far away he heard a boy's pained cries as a headmaster laid his stick to the boy's back. Bitter-cold gales blew in from the mountains, and he felt the relentless prodding of an investigator from Belgrave Square. He fell into a run. By the time he got through the trees, he was moving like a world class sprinter. But he couldn't seem to go fast enough. *They're after me, they're in me!* He reached the far end of the trees and stepped into the open air of the meadow. With his hands on his knees, he closed his eyes, expecting to see them, but, for the first time in a long time, his mind was quiet. *Have I done it? Are they gone?*

He waited. Still nothing. Only his voice was echoing in his mind. After a minute, he looked up at the moon creeping from behind a cloud. As it lit up the night sky, he cried out triumphantly, "Good riddance, bastards! Cobra is here to stay."

Chapter 17

Paris, France

Andrew Madison's first meeting as a member of the Morning Star organization had ended in disaster. As the grandson and reluctant heir to Harold Madison, co-founder of the group, he had hoped for at least some success. But after an arduous, ten-hour meeting, things had ended badly. Not only had the vessel they were charged with protecting gone missing, but the Caretaker, a man who had led the group for over forty years, had died in his effort to keep it safe.

Now what? Andrew wondered, as he laid his backpack on a chair in that same stale meeting room on the third floor of Paris's de Crillon Hotel. They had originally agreed to meet around one p.m., after Walter's lecture to the NATO attendees, but Andrew had received a memo to his room around twelve-thirty stating that their meeting had been moved to 7:00 p.m. That was it; no explanation. Though Andrew had been put off by the delay, he had welcomed the extra time to search for Maddi. He had spent the morning trying to find her, hoping to learn all that had happened to her since he had spoken to her five days earlier, as she had been about to leave a Paris hospital. She had told him then that she was going to the Baltic States to prepare for the NATO conference. NATO explained her return to Paris; it didn't explain how she had learned of the Morning Star. According to the members, it was one of the best kept secrets of all time, and he had had to marvel – once again – at his sister's ability to uncover such secrets. Though he was able to speak with her briefly when she had 'dropped by' unexpectedly toward the end of their meeting, there had been no time to actually discuss anything in depth. And, though he had lots of questions for his daring sister, his main concern was that she didn't look well...at all. She had lost weight, her cheeks were hollow, and her eyes had lost their sheen. Then again, she had been through a lot. More than once in the past month, someone had tried to kill her, and the last time had been with a hefty dose of poison.

He had found himself worried about her, so the minute the meeting had ended, he had returned to his room and had dialed her suite. She, too, was staying at the de Crillon, and was listed under her own name. But his calls had gone unanswered. He had tried her cellphone; those calls had gone straight to voicemail. Maddi was notorious for forgetting to charge her phone, so he had decided to go to her room. He had knocked several times, to no avail. He had called the concierge, who had refused to give him any information, in spite of Andrew pulling the *"It's a matter of life or death!"* card. So, he had taken a cab to where the NATO lectures were being held, and had spoken with a supervisor, asking if they kept a record of attendees. They did, but Maddi wasn't on any of the lists. Andrew had returned to the hotel, and, in an act of desperation, had resorted to bribing a maid, who had whispered in broken English that Maddi hadn't been to her room since check-in Saturday, except for a quick shower early Monday morning, which was just before she dropped in on the Morning Star meeting. He had ended the chat with the maid about ten minutes ago.

He checked his watch. *Six-fifty-eight.* The meeting was to start soon. He took off his coat and hung it over the back of his chair. He was expecting a knock on the door, but instead heard the beep from a keycard. Kauffold walked in and, with a solemn nod, sat in the same seat he had sat in last night across from Andrew. The old man's eyes had grown darker, his cheeks had lost their glow. His grief was palpable as he looked at Andrew and sighed. "I'm sorry for the delay of this meeting."

"What happened?"

"It was my fault. After we left this morning's meeting, I escorted my aide, Stanley, to the train station so he could head back to Chesham – no sense making the chap waste another day here – and I suddenly felt a need to tell Sean's wife of Sean's passing." He choked up. After a minute, he went on. "I got a seat on the 8:30 express to Lyon, and was able to at least spend a few hours with her." He sighed. "She took it surprisingly well, I have to say," he frowned, "...as if she was expecting it, actually."

Andrew said nothing, reminded of how much he didn't fit in in a world where a man's wife expected him to *not* come home. He cleared his throat. "I overheard you and Walter talking about her. I gather that she's quite ill?"

Kauffold nodded. "Cancer. It won't be long now." Andrew nodded solemnly. Kauffold shook his head, then sighed, his dark eyes suddenly intense. "But I'm afraid we have a new problem, Andrew." He sighed. "Walter...has gone missing."

"Missing?"

Kauffold nodded. "As you know, he was scheduled to speak at the NATO conference today at noon." He paused. "Well, he never made it to that lecture."

"Did he call to cancel?"

"No, but he did send the committee a handwritten note."

"What did it say?"

"Just that something had come up." Kauffold shook his head and sighed. "I checked with the hotel staff, but they refused to give me any information."

"Yes, they can be a bit stubborn."

The beep of a keycard interrupted them, and Johnny Canterbury waltzed into the room. He was still wearing his crisp suit and his cheesy grin. Andrew suddenly found the grin annoying. There was nothing to smile about, nothing at all. Johnny sat down next to Andrew. Kauffold told him about Walter.

"That's odd," Johnny said with a frown. "How did he sound when you last spoke with him, Ambassador?"

Kauffold sighed. "It was at the end of this morning's meeting. I was giving him back his cellphone; I guessed the lecture committee might need to reach him." He reached in his pocket and pulled out two cellphones. "Speaking of which," he handed Andrew and Simeon their phones, "...here you go. Please, use discretion." He went on. "Walter seemed okay. A bit stressed, but weren't we all?"

They nodded as they slid the phones in their pockets.

Andrew said, "Is there any reason to think something bad has happened?"

Kauffold frowned. "Actually, yes. Walter would never miss something as big as a NATO lecture, or even this meeting, without at last calling one of us to explain."

Johnny slapped his hand on the table. "Then we should notify the police."

Kauffold sat back and frowned. "Good god, man! Absolutely not. One thing you must understand, Johnny, is that no matter what, the existence of this group, or our connection to one another can never be revealed." He narrowed his eyes. "Do you understand?"

Johnny stiffened and gave a quick salute. "Aye, aye sir." He cleared his throat. "Well, I guess that means that it is up to us to find him."

"No...we can't go snooping around without risking exposure of the group." Kauffold sighed. "But I do have a friend that I've pulled in to help."

Johnny flinched. "I thought we couldn't tell anyone of our tie to one another."

"This friend isn't just 'anyone,'" Kauffold said, ignoring Johnny's cheekiness. "He's part of London's MI6, and I would trust the man with my life."

A cellphone vibrated, and Kauffold jumped, patting his vest awkwardly. "Blasted contraptions. I don't see how you all stand it." He pulled out a flip phone and fumbled for a pair of reading glasses. He slid them on his nose, and Andrew watched, amused, as Kauffold read through what was clearly a text.

Andrew grinned affectionately. "I take it you don't normally carry a phone?"

"No. I picked this up at the train station so my MI6 friend could reach me." Kauffold reread the text. Whatever it said, the words seemed to hit him hard.

Andrew frowned. "What's wrong, Arthur? Is it about Walter?"

Kauffold said nothing as he closed the phone and returned it to his pocket.

Andrew waited, but Kauffold offered no explanation. *I don't have time for this.* Andrew stood from his chair. He looked at Kauffold. "I'm sorry, Arthur, but I've got a lot going on, both with Maddi and back in America. And now that our mission has gone the way that it has, I don't really have much to offer. I certainly share your worries for Walter, as well as your grief over the loss of Sean," he paused, "...but I don't feel I'm of much use here." He put on his coat, grabbed his backpack from the chair and slung it over his shoulder. "I get that it was my duty to come here, but these problems are far bigger than anything I can help you with."

He had turned and was about to walk to the door, when Kauffold grabbed him by the arm. "Wait, Andrew. There's something you need to know." He paused. "I'm not sure if it has anything to do with Walter's disappearance, but you need to hear it."

Andrew tried to hide his frustration; he wasn't successful. "What on earth, Arthur, could your text say that I would need to hear? I really do need to get going."

Kauffold looked him in the eye and said evenly, "That text was from my friend at MI6. Apparently, a UK agent from Scotland Yard, Nigel Brooks, was murdered less than two hours ago in Lyon."

Andrew shook his head. "That's terrible, Ambassador, but what does it have to do with me? Or Walter?"

Kauffold frowned. "There's more. A Secret Service agent by the name of Spencer Seacroft was injured, as well, and is fighting for his life in a Lyon hospital." Andrew frowned. Seacroft's name sounded familiar, though he couldn't place him. He was about to again question the relevance, when Kauffold's voice took on a far more somber tone. "As I said, I'm not sure it has anything to do with Walter, but a man fitting Walter's description was seen in the square at about the same time. He and a woman were spotted leaving the scene with another man."

"I still don't see—"

Kauffold held up a hand. "Andrew, Seacroft and Brooks were your sister's bodyguards."

CHAPTER 18

Paris, France

Simeon was as nervous as a cat. But he couldn't show it; he had to maintain his carefree demeanor for the sake of the group...or what remained of it. But the news about Walter had stunned him. It was his job, after all, to keep tabs on the old man so that he could deliver him to Morningstar when the time was right. And he thought he had done so. He had stealthily followed Walter to his room after the first meeting had ended, had waited several minutes to make sure he didn't leave, and had gone so far as to bribe a front desk clerk to call him at once if the man checked out before his noon lecture. But Simeon hadn't heard from the clerk, which suggested that Walter hadn't checked out. *So, if he didn't check out, then where the hell is he?*

But it was the news about Andrew's sister, the annoying Senator Madison, that had truly floored him. He had had to refrain from clapping with joy upon hearing that her bodyguards were dead. *Maybe somebody got to that bitch, at last.*

The fact that Walter and Madison had possibly been together had been intriguing. Why? And why Lyon? As Andrew reacted to the news about his sister, Simeon did his best to probe for more details. There wasn't much. The man fitting Walter's description had been spotted in the square in the aftermath of some sort of mass-casualty event around five p.m.; the same event that had taken out Madison's two bodyguards. That was it. The man had left the square with a woman fitting Madison's description, and they had been escorted by an unidentified police officer.

143

"So, that's it? Maddi's bodyguards are dead and Maddi's missing?" Andrew said matter-of-factly. Kauffold nodded. Andrew pulled away from Kauffold's grip. With his backpack on his shoulder, he turned and walked to the door.

"Where are you going, Andrew?"

"To find my sister." Andrew left the room, slamming the door behind him.

The ambassador sighed as he ran his chubby hands through his thin white hair. Simeon shook his head. "Too much tragedy." He paused. "I do find it odd that Walter and the senator might have been together, don't you? And who was the cop?"

Kauffold said nothing, merely looking away, dismissing Simeon's – Johnny's – concerns as if he was nothing more than a bothersome child. *I hate that old man.* But it was clear that Kauffold was reeling, not only from the death of his friend, Sean, but from the disappearance of two people who were obviously very important to him.

Suddenly, Kauffold stood and walked to the door.

"Where are you going?" Simeon asked.

"To find Andrew and try to convince him to let the authorities handle this."

He left the room, leaving Simeon alone. *Asshole.* He looked at the closed door – the door that Andrew and Kauffold had both just stormed out of – and wondered if he should follow them. He sighed. *Andrew will move heaven and earth to find his sister.* He gave it another minute, then stood and stole out of the room. *And if what fatso says is true, then wherever the senator is, there, too, will be Walter.*

Chapter 19

Washington, DC

The Director of the Secret Service, Sam Allen wasn't a big man, but he seemed like it to anyone who met him. He had a square jaw and fierce brown eyes, and he was gruff and short-tempered. But underneath that rough exterior lay a gentle man; a thoughtful soul who felt things deeper than most. He did his best to hide it however, knowing his sternness was important to his role. There was a vital sense of order to the Service, and Allen felt that his harsh disposition was essential to keeping it intact. The men and women who served under him were responsible for the lives of those who led the Free World. It was imperative that they perform with automatic, disciplined responses. There was no room for error; no opportunity for do-overs.

But there were times, mostly when he was alone, that he felt overwhelmed by what he and his agents had been asked to do. There were so many bad people trying to take down so few good ones. *Like angels falling into Hell...and it's our job to keep them safe.* It was a tiring task with endless duties, and there were times when he wished he had chosen another career. *I could've been a cop; then I'd just have to protect a city.*

But Allen loved his work. Though, at times, it seemed impossible to fight so much evil, he knew that at the end of the day, his agents were making a difference. More than a senator, a Cabinet Secretary, or even the President, the Secret Service had an impact on the future of the country like no other entity. *We protect the very fiber of this nation.*

It was just after one in the afternoon, and he was sitting at his desk with a stale cup of coffee and a half-eaten ham sandwich. An American flag was draped behind him, with a photo of the President hanging next to it on the wall. He never shared his thoughts on the various presidents. Though he admired the current White House occupant, James Wilcox, it wouldn't matter if he didn't. He and the men and women of his organization would die for him – or her – regardless. *My job is to ensure that every one of my agents is ready and willing to do so...every hour of every day.*

He rubbed the back of his neck, then slammed a file on his desk. He stood and paced the room. He should have heard from Seacroft hours ago, and he was growing restless. Normally he would have called out the cavalry by now, but the agent's protectee, Senator Cynthia Madison, had proven to be unpredictable, to put it mildly. It wasn't unusual for Seacroft to call in late from time to time. *But never this late.*

His last contact with the agent had been the prior evening at midnight, which would have been six a.m. in France. They usually made contact four times a day – midnight, six a.m., noon, and six p.m. – to check in and go over Seacroft's schedule. This allowed for advance agents to do any preparatory work, as well as ensure that the protectee was alive and well. Allen should have gotten a call from Seacroft that morning at six – which would have been noon in Paris – then again at noon, which would be six p.m. in France. There had been no calls. He was trying to decide if he should call the Paris prefect, the French National Police, or maybe even Interpol. *So much needless drama if Madison is simply pulling another one of her stunts.*

He had decided to give it until six p.m. – midnight in Paris – to allow Seacroft time to 'catch up' with the call schedule, but six was a long time away. He reviewed the itinerary his agent had given him when he had called at midnight. They had gotten to Paris late Saturday morning in order for Senator Madison to prepare for the NATO conference. A friend of hers had taken ill, so they had planned to spend most of Sunday – yesterday – at the American hospital outside Paris. They had not yet made plans for Monday, but Seacroft had assured Allen he would call the minute he knew. *"We'll stay in Paris, for now"* he had told his boss.

Allen had tried to call Seacroft at eleven – two hours ago – which would have been five p.m. in Paris, but the call hadn't gone through. That in and of itself had alarmed him. He had then tried the Paris hotel and, though they still listed the senator as a guest, the concierge hadn't seen her since her check-in Sunday at noon; over thirty hours ago. The Paris hospital had been no help. *"We're sorry, sir, but we have no information on your agent or the senator."* So, now he was faced with a decision; does he alert the entire French brigade to what might simply be an unexpected change of plans, or does he do nothing and sit tight, hoping Seacroft will contact him soon.

There was a knock on the door. "Sir, there's a phone call for you."

"Send it through." The phone rang and he picked it up. "Sam Allen here."

A strong French accent came over the line. "Monsieur Allen. My name is Inspector Gagneux, and I oversee France's Directorate-General for External Security. I have some bad news, I'm afraid."

Allen frowned. The General Directorate for External Security was France's equivalent to the CIA. *Why are they calling me?* he wondered as he fell into his chair. "Go ahead."

"I am sorry to report that one of your agents has been critically wounded in Lyon."

"One of my agents?"

"*Oui,* sir. A Spencer Seacroft."

147

Allen's stomach knotted. "In Lyon? What the hell's he doing there?" Without waiting for an answer, he added, "How serious?"

"I'm sorry, sir, but it does not look good. He was shot in the neck and the bullet nicked his carotid artery. The doctors have done all that they could...now it is just a matter of waiting to see if he will recover."

"What the hell happened?"

"We are not sure. There was a shoot-out this afternoon at Place Bellecour. Your agent was wounded and several others were killed. It appears a prominent U.S. senator is missing...I am guessing that she was your agent's protectee?"

Hell yeah, she was! "Her name is Cynthia Madison."

"That is what we have determined from the eye-witness."

"You have an eye-witness?"

"Yes, sir. Actually, there are several. But only one was able to relay the sequence of events logically. He owns a café in the square. He recognized the senator and gave us what little information we have."

Allen cleared his throat. "Which hospital was Seacroft taken to?"

"Saint Luc, sir. Is there anything else you would like me to do?"

Hell yes! Make my agent well, find the prick that did this, and find Madison! "I'd like whatever you have on the shooter, as well as anything you can find on Madison's whereabouts." He paused. "And I'll need the name of that eye witness."

"Certainly, sir. I will have my men get the information to you right away. I will call you in an hour with an update. Is that satisfactory?"

No! I need answers now! "Yeah, sure. I'll give you my sat-phone number. It'll work anywhere." He gave the man the number. "By the way, there was another agent with Seacroft; a man by the name of Brooks. Nigel Brooks."

There was a pause. "I'm sorry, sir. Mr. Brooks is dead."

Allen closed his eyes.

"Monsieur?"

"Yeah, okay, just call me when you have something."

He hung up the phone and stared at his desk. Brooks was dead and Seacroft was fighting for his life...*in Lyon!* He pounded his fist. *What the hell happened over there?* He stood and resumed his pacing. He had to do something. He couldn't wait for a French police force, which he knew nothing about, to do the work that belonged to him and his agency. He needed to speak to the hospital administrator where they had taken Seacroft, and he had to get some men to Lyon right away.

He went to the doorway and yelled for his aide. An eager young man was there in seconds. "Yes sir?"

"Connect me with the guy in charge at Saint Luc Hospital in France."

"Yes sir."

"Then I need you to find me two men to travel to Lyon immediately."

"Yes sir. Anyone in particular?"

Allen sighed. The assignment would require two of his best agents. "Yeah, get me Cravens and Cross."

The agent nodded. "How soon should they be ready, sir?"

"Within the hour. Arrange for air transport. Let the men know that they may not return for a while."

"Yes sir." The aide hurried off to his tasks while Allen continued to pace. He thought of Seacroft and choked. He felt as if he had practically raised the boy, taking him under his wing when he had learned the young man's tragic story of his parents' deaths. Seacroft was good – one of the best – but he

149

had a tendency to get too close to those he was protecting. As Allen paced the office, he couldn't help but wonder, *Had Seacroft gotten too close? Was this a case where his judgment was skewed by his emotional tie to Madison?* Suddenly he wanted to kick himself. *Of course, it was!* He should never have let Seacroft watch over the appealing senator. How could anyone *not* get close to her?

He stopped and leaned against his desk. He rubbed his forehead as he recalled the night not that long ago when another agent, Larry Moses, had been killed in a Providence hotel room. Even then, after Madison had been through so much – her life had been threatened and her agent had been murdered in the bedroom next to her – she had still been gracious and kind. There was no doubt in his mind that Seacroft had let her unwittingly lure him into a bad situation.

There was a knock on the door. The aide leaned in and informed Allen that the hospital administrator was on the line.

Allen picked up the receiver. "This is Sam Allen, Director of the U.S. Secret Service."

"Oui, Monsieur. How may I help?"

"You have my agent, Spencer Seacroft, in your hospital. I need you to keep a close eye on him. Don't let anyone know where he is; not the newspapers or TV. I want to know the minute there's a change in his condition. You got it?"

"Oui, Monsieur. I will keep him out of the news, and I will notify you at once if there is any change."

"Is there a guard at his door?"

"Oui, Monsieur. Inspector Gagneux assigned one immediately upon his arrival."

"Good. Keep me posted." Allen slammed down the phone. His stomach was in knots as he thought about Brooks dead and Seacroft fighting for his life in a foreign hospital. Both men were capable, accomplished agents...so, what happened over there? He closed his eyes as a chill ran through him. *And where the hell's the senator?*

Chapter 20

London, England

"Carter, get in here."

The dutiful Scotland Yard officer ran into the room. "Yes, Inspector?"

"Get me an update on CIA Agent Clarkson. He's in a hospital outside Paris."

The man nodded and hurried off to make the call.

Scotland Yard's Chief Inspector, Sir Lionel Pritchard, sighed as he leaned back in his chair. He had learned on his way back from France, that Roger Clarkson had been kidnapped by Cobra. Just before his abduction, he and Pritchard had been investigating the murder of a woman in Calais whose death had all the markings of the renowned killer. Pritchard had gone there in hopes of uncovering a clue, and had been only slightly surprised to see Roger there, as well. They had conferred briefly, and, from what Pritchard could gather, Roger had been kidnapped from a bar just minutes later...*with me only a hundred yards away!* Alarmed by the news, Pritchard had instantly put in a call to Roger's father, Hank, the Deputy Director of America's Homeland Security, whom he had gotten to know after the attack at the Queen's Ball. He had been relieved to learn that Roger had been found alive. The doctors weren't sure if he would make it, however, and it had left Pritchard incensed. Though he hadn't known the agent long, he liked him. It was as if their common pursuit of Cobra had bonded them in a way few would understand. But it had also made him curious. Why had Cobra spared Roger's life? He rarely left his victims alive. There must have been a reason. What had he gained by taking, then leaving, the CIA agent?

He leaned back and rubbed his eyes. He was tired. So much had happened in only a week's time, and he couldn't help but feel responsible. Though Cobra had been the culprit for nearly all of it, Pritchard felt as if he had failed...as if he himself had injected poison into the victims...as if he himself had bled them to death.

He undid his collar, a rare act by the Inspector. He had spent the entire weekend in Calais investigating Cobra's murder of the young woman, and had gotten back just over an hour ago. Greeted by a pile of telephone messages, he had barely gotten through the first few. He stared at the pile, then sat back and tugged at his thin silver-gray mustache. *I'm getting too old for this.*

Pritchard had held his role as Chief Inspector for the past five years. Prior to that, he'd been twice-decorated for going above and beyond the call of duty. None of it mattered now; Cobra had managed to put all his years of service to shame. The man had killed mercilessly, his victims ranging from the obscure Lida Mae McLeod, to the well-known Secretary of State, Jane Harper. He winced. *My date for the evening, no less.* He wanted Cobra more than life itself, and he knew it may come to that; he may die in his effort to take him down. *As long as I get him, so be it.* He didn't fear death; he feared a life of leaving unanswered what had happened on his watch.

He grimaced as he recalled the beautiful Jane Harper dancing in his arms at the Queen's Ball. She had been moving elegantly with the passion of the dance, holding him longer than necessary as they finished a well-executed *fleckeryll.* She had then fallen to the floor, struck by a poisoned dart from Cobra's arsenal. The toxin had killed her instantly. As Pritchard had stared at her pained eyes looking up at him, he had sworn on his life that he would find and kill the bastard who had murdered her.

But so far, he had failed. And the only other man who shared his obsession, CIA agent Clarkson, was fighting for his life in a Paris hospital, a victim of the very man they were trying to find. Which was why he was eager to go back to Paris...to visit Roger, then hopefully find – and kill – Cobra.

And if it wasn't for this blasted Edinburgh conference, I'd be on my way. Pritchard sighed as he stared at the packet on his desk. The conference, set to begin tomorrow morning, had been arranged months earlier by a UN commission looking into the contamination of Dalgety Bay. The bay, located about twenty miles north of Edinburgh, had been a holding ground for World War II aircraft. The planes, left there after the war, had control dials made of radium, and remnants from the dials were seeping into the soil. The radioactivity had reached intolerable levels. The Prime Minister had requested that Pritchard join the scientists at the conference, hoping the Inspector could use his high regard and his influence to keep the commission from designating the site a toxic wasteland. It would be a damaging blow to tourism if a Scottish coastline was deemed a hazardous waste site. *"Keep 'em from ruining the bay, Pritchard,"* the Prime Minister had said. Pritchard hadn't wanted to go, even before everything that had happened last week. But he had had no say in the matter, a point the Prime Minister had made crystal clear. Pritchard's only hope was that the meeting would end quickly, after which he would catch the first train to Paris.

He tugged again on his mustache as he shifted in his seat, his slight frame barely filling the chair. He had never felt so tired. He looked forward to getting a good night's sleep on the overnight train to Edinburgh. It was due to leave at 11:00 that night out of Euston Station. There was nothing more relaxing than the rhythm of the train, and he hoped to rest well, perhaps for the first time in weeks.

155

He leaned forward and ran his fingers through his silver-black hair. He stared at the messages. *Time to go through the phone calls, Pritchard.* He was startled by a knock on the door. "Yes?"

"Sir, there's a Professor Klein on the line. Says 'e has information about the Cobra."

Pritchard's eyes widened. "Put him through." He leaned forward with his hand on the phone. It rang and he lifted the receiver. "Hello."

A deep voice with a thick Austrian accent said, "Is this Chief Inspector Lionel Pritchard of Scotland Yard?"

"Yes, and you are?"

"Gustav Klein. I am a professor at the University of Vienna. I'm calling because I have information that may be helpful in your hunt for Cobra."

"Gustav Klein?" Pritchard jotted the name on his blotter.

"Yes. I studied under Dr. James Samuels at the University of Vienna. He and I became close during that time, sharing an appreciation for the teachings of Sigmund Freud. I hadn't spoken with him in years. That is, until yesterday."

Pritchard wrote down Samuels' name, as well; it looked familiar. *One of the messages while I was in France!* He rummaged through the messages. He found the memo regarding Samuels, but all it had was the man's name, and a request for Pritchard to call him. *Was this what he wanted to discuss?*

The professor continued. "He called me – from where, I don't know – and told me he was involved in a difficult case. Back in school, we used to discuss complex cases, so I thought nothing of it...until he said, *'I think I may have been talking to the Cobra.'* You can imagine my surprise, Inspector. In our line of work, we occasionally encounter murderers and thieves, but Cobra is much more than an ordinary criminal. I encouraged Samuels to talk about the case, but he refused to elaborate."

Pritchard frowned. "Then why did he call you?"

"That's what I asked. He said, *'I will soon need your help, Gustav. And I will need the help of one other man, Inspector Pritchard from the Yard.'* He then asked that I speak with you and try to encourage you to join me."

"Join you where?"

"I'm not quite sure. He said something about southern France, but promised to call tomorrow morning with more details."

Pritchard snorted. *This is insane.* But it was the first lead he had gotten since the Secretary's murder; he needed to at least play it out. "With all due respect, sir, I'll need more than that to convince me to join you."

There was a pause. "There's an item I can share. I think it will convince you."

"What is it?"

"I received it in last night's post. I can only show you in person. I'm in Brussels at a conference, and I am prepared to travel to London tonight. I could get there by 10:30 your time...if that's not too late."

Pritchard was scheduled to leave for Edinburgh on the 11:00 train. He didn't want to miss this chance to possibly learn more about Cobra, but the Prime Minister would have his head if he failed to show for his meeting the next morning. Somehow, he had to do both. "It's not too late at all." He hesitated. "Professor Klein, this will seem a bit irregular, but how would you feel about accompanying me to Edinburgh? I'm leaving tonight for a meeting in the morning. We can discuss the case on the way up, sleep on the train, then wait for Samuels' call." He paused. "I'm hoping the meeting will end by noon. If your information is compelling, and Samuels truly has a lead, then we can leave straightaway from

Edinburgh. I can get us a plane to southern France, or to anywhere in the world for that matter."

There was a pause. "Why, that's a splendid idea. I'll be there by 11:00."

"Good. I'll have a man pick you up at Heathrow and bring you to Euston."

Another pause. "Let me meet you at your train. No need to trouble your staff."

"Whatever you say, Professor. I'll see you at Euston Station by eleven." He paused. "And don't worry about your ticket. I'll take care of it."

"Excellent. Thank you, Inspector. I will see you soon."

Pritchard hung up the receiver, grabbed a pencil, and underlined Klein's name with several bold strokes. *A strange call...a trick, perhaps?* He lifted the receiver, pushed a button, and said, "Carter, see what you can find on a Professor Gustav Klein from the University of Vienna."

"Yes sir."

"And check on a Dr. James Samuels, as well."

"Yes sir."

Pritchard flipped through the pile of phone messages. He saw that several had been left by Samuels. He looked at the most recent, which had come through at eight that morning. The message requested that Pritchard call Samuels at once...that he had "vital information." Pritchard reached for his desk phone and dialed the number. It went straight to voicemail. He cleared his throat. "Uh...this is Chief Inspector Lionel Pritchard from Scotland Yard returning your call. Please get back to me as soon as you can." He rattled off the numbers for his cellphone and for Scotland Yard and ended the call.

He leaned back, trying to imagine what sort of information the doctor might have for him. He had worked with psychiatrists on cases over the years, but had always found them to be a bit odd; rarely had they been very helpful. Would Samuels be any different? If what Klein had told him was true, he would soon find out.

He glanced at his watch. It was almost seven. He had no obligations until he left for the train, other than to get through the mound of paperwork on his desk. His stomach growled. *I'll get to it after I grab a bite to eat.*

He picked up his hat and walked out the door. "I'm going to supper, Carter. If Dr. Samuels calls again, put him through to my private cellphone."

The aide nodded and Pritchard left the office. He walked down three flights of stairs and strode out the back door to the street. The sun had set about an hour ago, and he breathed in, enjoying the briskness of the cool March air. He nodded a salute to the moonlight as it formed shadows on the sidewalk...*like sentries standing watch.*

He walked several blocks to his favorite diner, a place known as Harry's to the locals. It was off the beaten path, which meant there would be few tourists. That suited Pritchard just fine; he thought best when not inundated with people. A hot meal and a pint of ale would give him a chance to process the odd call from the professor.

Klein had said that Samuels would provide details regarding a location "...*when he calls me tomorrow morning.*" The entire matter seemed odd, indeed, and he would be eager to see how things went with the Viennese professor.

He reached the café, leaving the shadows at the door as he went to his usual spot at a table in the back. He ordered his favorite; bangers and mash, with a half pint of McEwen Ale. He hoped a drink or two would relax him. He was certain that he would soon have a stroke if he didn't find a way to calm down.

He laid a napkin on his lap as his ale was set in front of him. He sipped it; the taste alone was relaxing. After a few minutes, his meal came and he took a bite. He relaxed a bit more. He took another sip of ale, savoring it as he leaned forward and spooned in a second mouthful of food. He was beginning to feel content. The moment was quickly lost, however – as all moments of contentment had been – by a memory of the Queen's Ball. *Quit thinking about it, Pritchard.*

He chugged more of the ale as he tried to imagine what the Viennese professor might share. It seemed odd that the man knew of him merely through a conversation with Samuels, a psychiatrist whom Pritchard had never even heard of, let alone met. It didn't matter. Klein might have information that would lead to Cobra; Pritchard had no choice but to follow the lead.

He took another bite of sausage and looked outside. It was as if he was a thousand miles from London, a thousand miles from murder, a thousand miles from the deeds of Cobra. How he wished he could stay there, removed from it all, spending his days in that fleeting quietude. If only there was a place where he could go to truly find that peace. He smiled. Fortunately, there was. He had purchased a small plot of land near Dover. It looked out on the white cliffs, and, on the rare occasion when he could get away, he would go there and sit on the spot where he would someday build a home. It had been his dream for years. *When I'm done here,* he thought with a sigh.

He finished his dinner and took a final sip of ale, regretful that his repast had come to an end. Big Ben rang out eight chimes as Pritchard laid several bills on the table and left the diner. He had a lot to do before he boarded the train.

Fortunately, he kept a travel bag with two nights worth of clothes and essentials at his office. There was no one to go home to; no one to bid goodbye before he left town. He had made the decision early on to not bring a wife and family into his line of work; he didn't even own a dog. It was just him...all by himself. His thoughts went back to Jane Harper and he sighed. For one brief moment, he hadn't been alone; for a single night, he had had a companion. One perfect night that had ended in tragedy.

He picked up his pace, reaffirming his vow to catch Cobra. As he hurried back to the Yard, he thought again of his small plot of land outside Dover. It overlooked the North Sea and Pritchard felt lucky to have acquired such a spot. It had been covered with brambles, but he had hired two young men to help him clear it, and the half acre was now the loveliest place on earth. He had envisioned the house he would build so many times...it was as if the place already existed. He imagined walking through an oversized front door, past a wooden bench that would sit in the foyer. He could almost feel the welcoming ease of the overstuffed chair that would wait for him in the parlor at the end of each day, and he could practically taste the tea and toast he would enjoy every morning as he sat at the kitchen table looking out at the sea. *I will go there when I'm finished.* Would he ever be finished? *Yes,* he thought. *When I've captured – and killed – the Cobra.*

He reached the Yard, suddenly feeling tired and old. He sighed as he trudged up the stairs, saying to no one in particular, "And it can't come soon enough."

Chapter 21

Lyon, France

Maddi hadn't moved from Henderson's side. Though he could barely speak, his presence made her feel content. She could almost pretend that things were as they had been before the hotel fire, before the attempts on her life, before Henderson had become a changed man...a man capable of killing other men. But something was terribly wrong with him. It was beyond the beatings she felt certain that Cobra had given him; it was as if he was drugged, or maybe even ill. She did her best to look him over, her years as a physician coming back to her as she listened to his breathing and checked his pulse. Though the pulse was slow, just 54 beats a minute, it was steady; it wouldn't account for his lethargy. *What did you do to him, Cobra?*

Cobra. She had heard of the assassin, but had never dreamed that she would be a victim of his insanity. And he was insane; that much was clear from his chilling rant. As he had gone back and forth between the ghosts in his mind, and had then run from the dungeon in a crazed fit, she had tried to square his behavior with the fact that he was a Henderson. How could that murderous lunatic have come from the bloodline of the two men next to her? The Hendersons weren't just kind and respectable; they had spent their lives risking everything for the betterment of others. It made no sense.

She had watched Cobra closely; the way his eyes had narrowed when he had looked at Walter, the anguish on his face as he had lost himself to specters that had seemed to appear out of nowhere. There had been only one trait she recognized...only one quality that could qualify him as a Henderson...*the eyes.* They were strong and defiant, and, though they were different colors, and lacked the kindness shared by the two men with her now, they were Henderson eyes...and it made her shudder.

How many times had the madman called Walter his father? At least four, and it was killing her to not know what tied the two men to one another. Walter had referred to Cobra as Mark, suggesting that he knew him in an entirely different way than the rest of the world. Cobra had said that Walter had slept with Cobra's mother. Was it true? If so, why? Walter had a beautiful wife and he was highly respected, not only in America, but around the world. Why would such a man feel the need to cheat?

The questions were churning inside her, but she said nothing, simply sitting in the dark with Henderson's head in her lap. She combed through his hair, then stroked his cheek and smiled. *He's here; he's really here.* But he looked rough. His cheeks were drawn, his hair dirty, his chin covered with stubble. The stubble did, however, soften his jawline, making him look more like the man she had met so many years ago. But he was nothing like that man; not any more.

She looked up and saw Walter standing only a foot away. He was staring at his son. Why hadn't he spoken to him? What was he afraid of? Maddi swallowed. *He's afraid of what he doesn't know about the last four years of his son's life.* She understood. Just reading a few pages of Henderson's journal had convinced her that — whatever he had done — it wasn't good.

She nodded at him and smiled. "Come here, Walter."

The older man looked down at her, his light blue eyes charcoal gray in the darkness of the dungeon. A steady stream of moonlight spilling through the window helped her to see his features, but she was having a hard time reading his face, grasping what he was thinking after verifying with his own eyes that Martin was alive.

He took a deep breath, then knelt down next to his son. He looked at Maddi, then reached a shaking hand to Martin's shoulder. He was trying not to cry, but tears finally came as he stared at the son that he thought he had lost. Neither man said a word as Walter kept his hand on Martin's shoulder, then finally bent down and hugged him.

Maddi tried to imagine what it must feel like to lose your child to tragedy, honor his life as you bury his memory, do your best to move on, and then – like a bolt from the blue – discover that he hadn't really died. *A part of me would be so angry.*

As if on cue, Walter let go of his son and sat back on his knees. His voice caught as he said, with a mix of desperation and anger, "Why didn't you tell me?"

Henderson whispered, "You wouldn't approve...of who I became."

Maddi shook her head. She looked at Walter and frowned. "I didn't know, either." She thought it might comfort him to learn that Martin hadn't only failed to tell his parents, but had also failed to tell the woman he loved.

The reaction was the opposite, however. Walter jumped up, bristling as he paced from one end of the cell to the other. After a minute he stopped. He looked down at Martin and, in a voice still angry, yet filled with grief, he said, "I wouldn't care if you joined forces with the Devil, himself, Martin. To have you back – flawed – would have been better than what we went through."

Henderson forced his eyes open, but it was clear that even that simple gesture took nearly all his strength. He tried to sit up. He couldn't and fell back against Maddi. She held him tight, overcome by how familiar he felt, yet how much like a stranger he seemed, as well.

He looked at her, then at his father. "I...I don't think you get it, Dad." His voice cracked. "I *did* join forces with the Devil." He closed his eyes. "I did."

Walter fell to his knees and pulled him close, holding him so tight that Maddi thought he might hurt him. Martin said nothing, doing his best to hug his father with his weak arms. Walter finally let go, laying him once again in Maddi's lap.

"It's okay, son. I'm sorry to be angry," he said as he wiped his eyes. "But I meant what I said. I don't care what you've done. I will love you regardless."

Martin looked up at Maddi and her heart broke. She could see it; the shame in his eyes, as if he was saying, *"No...neither one of you will be able to love me when you realize what I've done."*

She bent closer and whispered in his ear, "I swear to you, *it doesn't matter.*"

He closed his eyes, and she stroked his hair. She looked at Walter and sighed. "It's none of my business, Walter, but I have to ask. Is Cobra truly your...son?"

Walter stood and walked to the window. He looked up, the moonlight outlining his features as he whispered, "Yes."

Maddi felt an overwhelming sense of grief for the man, unable to even fathom such a scenario. "You don't need to say more," adding, "...I'm sure it's been hard."

He nodded, a shadow on the wall nodding with him. "Yes, it has. For his mother, as well."

Maddi felt Henderson's entire body tense. She tried to imagine what he felt as he heard his father speak so candidly about another woman. *Cobra – a crazed killer – was born from a lie.* Suddenly she wondered: *Does Dora know?*

As if reading her mind, Walter said, "Dora doesn't know...not about...*him,* anyway." He grimaced. "But she knows about Nenita."

Again, Maddi felt Henderson tense. She ran her fingers over his cheek. "I'm sure it's complicated," she said, as she thought of the cop from her past. "Things are rarely simple," she paused, "...not the things that matter, anyway."

Walter nodded as he looked at his son. "Martin, I know you've hated me for this chapter in my life. I've hated myself. But Nenita is sick; she has fought cancer for over a decade and I couldn't abandon her." He turned away. "Besides, I love her."

Henderson opened his eyes, too spent to be angry. "What about Mom?" he asked, his raspy voice a whisper. "You can't love two people at the same time, Dad."

In unison, Walter and Maddi said, "Oh, but you can."

Henderson closed his eyes. "I guess it's hard for me to know...I've loved only one." He squeezed Maddi's hand; his hands were ice cold. She held them to her chest and rubbed them. *He'll die if we don't get him out of here soon.* She pulled his jacket more snuggly over his shoulders and chest, then looked at Walter standing beneath the window. "We need to find a way out of here."

Henderson's teeth were chattering, as he said weakly, "The...window...is the only way out. The door is...locked from the outside. Cobra...has the key."

Walter took off his jacket, walked over, and laid it over Henderson's legs and feet. He went to the door and pushed against it, flinching as the clang of a metal lock filled the silence. He walked back to the window and stared at the opening.

Maddi watched him, awed by the strength of the Henderson traits and how solidly they had passed from father to son. In the shadows, Walter could have been Martin; same face, same eyes, same stance as he prepared to do battle with the impossible. Her heart ached for the man who had been reunited with his son, only to learn that they would both soon die at the hand of his other son. *Like a Shakespearian tragedy.*

Suddenly her eyes lit up. She laid Henderson's head gently on the ground and kissed his forehead, then stood and walked over to Walter. She looked up at the window and nodded. "I think I have an idea."

CHAPTER 22

Somewhere over France

The plane couldn't get there quickly enough. Jenny Clarkson, ex-wife to Hank and mother to Roger, had been flying for over seven hours, and she was certain it was the longest seven hours of her entire 43 years of life. *Come on, land already!* Though she was small, about five-three, she still felt cramped in the tiny seat. She could only imagine what a bigger person must feel.

Hank had given her little information in his phone call, telling her only that Roger had had '*...a run-in with a bad guy,*' and that she should take the first plane to Paris. He had assured her that Roger was fine, but Jenny had known Hank over half his life; she recognized the worry in his voice. There had been no flights available until morning, and she had left Cleveland-Hopkins at 7:00 a.m. It was an eight-hour flight and, with the time-change, she wasn't scheduled to land at De Gaulle until around nine p.m. *Dear God, don't let anything happen to him before I can get to him.*

Jenny wasn't prone to hysterics; she had always been the calm one. When Roger fell out of a tree or wrecked his bike, it had been her job to take him to the emergency room and wait by his side with a smile and a reassuring nod as the doctors did whatever was needed. Hank would show up later; well after the sutures had been placed and the bandages wrapped, and that had been fine. She had taken in stride the demands on her husband because of his work, and she had become the sole caretaker of crises, the chief overseer of calamities. But this was different; it was Hank who had called her and had told her to get to Paris – as soon as possible – to be with Roger. She had pressed him for details, but he had

169

refused to share anything more. So, of course, she knew...*something serious has happened to our son.*

She brushed light brown bangs from her forehead, aware that she probably looked horrendous. It couldn't be helped. Worrying about her hair was not a priority when her son's life was at stake. Was his life at stake? Was he hovering near death, or had he merely been injured and wanted his mother at his side? She shook her head and sighed. Never had she felt so useless; so out of touch with the needs of her family. She had known when Roger joined the CIA there was a chance he might get hurt, but she had imagined he would be close by; at least near enough that she could get to him within an hour or two. After all, looking after him had been her job for all his life; the thought of him hurting without her there felt like a knife to the heart...as if she had failed in her duties...as if she had abandoned him to the unrelenting cruelties of the world. *Hurry up, plane!*

Finally, the captain came on the loud speaker and said that they were nearing De Gaulle. She put up her seat back and her tray table and waited anxiously to land. She looked out, suddenly sad as she saw the bright lights of Paris. It had always been her dream to go to Paris – with Hank – but the timing had never been right. In their early years, they were too busy with Roger, medical school, and adjusting to the sudden advent of a family. Once they were in a position to take such a trip, their relationship wasn't where it needed to be. So, she had never been, and now, here she was, finally in Paris, but wishing so badly that it was under different circumstances.

Hopefully Roger was fine; hopefully Hank had been telling her the truth and her son simply wanted to see her because he loved her and wanted her at his side as he recovered from his 'mild injuries.' *Baloney!* The only reason Hank would call her and ask her to fly halfway around the world was if Roger was in trouble...*real* trouble. Her hands began to shake. She gripped them in her lap. *Calm down, Jenny.*

The plane hit the runway and she clung to the armrest as it sped toward the terminal. It slowed, and she felt her heart speed up. *I'm close, Roger...hang on.* They reached the gate and she waited impatiently for passengers to unload. It was all she could do to not shove past them as she stepped into the aisle and allowed herself to be herded off the plane. She practically ran through the terminal, her carryon her only piece of luggage as she followed signs to customs. Her bag held a change of clothes, a toothbrush, and a comb...all she would need to tend to her son.

She stopped at a bathroom and splashed water on her face. As she looked in the mirror at her tired eyes and pale skin, she sighed. She was getting older and, though she had aged well, she looked nothing like the young girl who had fallen in love with Hank Clarkson so many years ago. They had been in middle school, and she had just moved to town. The wrinkles by her eyes were absent then; the lines in her forehead years away. They were simpler times, and oh, how she longed for them now....

"You dropped your paper."

Jenny Wilson turned to see who had spoken to her. He had bent over to pick up the paper and was holding it in front of him. He was handsome in a quirky sort of way. His brown hair was curly, long, and messy. The eyes were the same brown and they sparkled when he grinned. He was muscular; probably an athlete. The last thing she needed was some jock taking pity on the new girl at school. She gave a quick smile, grabbed the paper, and said, 'Thank you.' She turned and hurried to class.

She entered the classroom and found her seat, doing her best to focus on the lecture. But she found her mind wandering to the curly-haired boy with the warm smile. Finally, in an effort to distract her from thinking of him, she threw open her notebook, and began to copy – word for word – every sentence from her science book. Fifty minutes went by, the bell rang, and she walked out of class and to her locker. She saw the same boy standing beside it; she pretended not to notice. He grinned as she approached. She said coolly, "What are you doing here?"

He laughed and she felt her heart skip a beat. He said, "I thought you might need help getting to the next class." He paused. "You seem to have a problem holding onto your papers." He knelt behind her and picked up another piece of paper she had dropped. She took the paper, glaring at him as she stuffed it in a folder. She grabbed a book from the locker, then turned and walked away. He followed her, clearly undaunted. "You wanna' join me for lunch?" he asked.

She practically snorted. "Don't you have a group of ball players to sit with?"

He chuckled. "Not any more. I either eat with you or I eat alone."

She stopped and looked at him. His eyes were dark, yet warm, his smile welcoming. She could feel her hands shaking, and she gripped the book tighter as she turned and walked away. Then, over her shoulder she said, "Well, I wouldn't want you to eat alone..."

Jenny sighed as she patted the water from her face. She and Hank had been in love once, and from that had come Roger. And, because of their love for him, they had remained close. Though neither one seemed to want things to go back to the way they had been, sometimes, in the middle of the night, Jenny would wonder about him. She would hope his life was going well...that he was happy. What did he think about when he thought of her...did he even think of her?

An announcement overhead startled her and she threw the paper towel in the trash. She left the bathroom and walked to customs. She got through with little difficulty, and was soon walking out of the terminal into a cold Parisian night. Her heart ached as she saw the Eiffel Tower in the distance. Yes, she had always longed to see Paris. But not in the snapshots she was about to see on her way to her injured son. No, she had wanted to *feel* Paris...slow and easy, with plenty of time, maybe even a little romance. But it would have to wait. There was no time...and there was certainly no romance.

She waited in line for a cab. When her turn came, she slid in back of an old gray taxi and said, "American hospital. Hurry please."

The cabby pulled away, zipping between cars to get to the freeway. They drove west on highway A1, and Jenny undid her purse to put away her passport. As she opened her wallet, she saw a wrinkled photo hiding behind a piece of plastic. Roger's young face smiled up at her and she smiled back, tears stinging her cheeks as she did her best to not let the driver see her cry. The picture was of their family. Eleven-year-old Roger was sitting happily between her and Hank. All three were smiling for the camera, but their eyes weren't smiling; at least not hers or Hank's. The picture was taken just before the divorce. Though the family would soon be split, Jenny had wanted the photo to serve as a reminder of what they had been. Roger was only a boy, and, though the divorce had hurt him deeply, she found herself suddenly longing for the days when the worst that could happen to him was a fall from a tree, a skinned knee from a bike wreck, or a broken heart from the splitting of his parents. Now, her beautiful boy followed criminals around the world, and someone had gotten a hold of him and had hurt him. She choked as she stared at the picture; what she wouldn't give to go back. She wiped a tear and said to the driver. "How long?"

The driver looked at her in the rearview mirror and smiled sadly. He seemed to understand. "Not long at all, Madame."

She nodded and forced a smile. As she wiped another tear from her cheek, she thought, *but will it be soon enough?*

Chapter 23

Lyon, France

Walter looked at Maddi. "What's your plan?"

Maddi had been pacing the dungeon, periodically staring up at the window, saying nothing as she focused on the bars. Finally, she turned to Walter and nodded. "I'll need your shirt."

He hesitated, then removed Maddi's scarf from where she had tied it over his wounded shoulder. He let it fall to the floor. He then took off the white dress shirt he had been wearing for the past two days, and handed it to Maddi.

Maddi flinched when she saw the wound on his shoulder. Even with the limitations of moonlight, she could see that Cobra's bullet had done quite a bit of damage. She tugged gently at the edges to see if it gapped. "It needs sutures."

"It doesn't even hurt, Maddi. Let's get on with it."

She nodded. "Now I need some blood."

"I've got plenty of that."

He was about to scrape open the scab on his shoulder when Maddi said, "No, you've been hurt enough." Before he could stop her, she scraped her hand against the rough edge of the dungeon's wall. She ignored the pain as she took her bloodied hand and wrote "SOS" on the white shirt. She fanned the shirt to let it dry, then looked again at Walter's shoulder. "I don't know if I can do the next part."

Walter frowned. "What do you mean?"

"I need to climb onto your shoulders." She paused. "But I'm afraid I'll tear open your wound."

"I don't care, Maddi. Do what you have to."

175

Maddi sighed. "I think I can do it without putting pressure directly on it."

"I'm sure you can," he said, as he walked closer to the window. He bent his knees and offered his hand. Maddi grabbed it as she kicked off her shoes. He pulled her onto his thighs. "Ready?" he asked. She nodded as she draped the shirt around her neck. He took her other hand, then pulled her onto his shoulders. "You okay?"

"Ye—yes. How about you?"

"I'm...fine." He edged closer to the window.

Maddi could hear him grunt with the effort but he didn't complain. Though she could feel the strong muscles under her feet, he was an older man and it made her uneasy, especially with his injury. But there was no other option; Henderson was ill, maybe dying, and Cobra would soon return and kill them all if they didn't find a way out. She grabbed onto the bars of the window for balance, feeling a wave of deference as he said nothing under the weight of her fidgeting body. "I'm so sorry, Walter."

Through gritted teeth he said, "I'm...okay."

She grabbed the shirt from around her neck and tied a sleeve around one of the bars. She then tossed the shirt through the window, making sure the blood-stained letters showed to the outside. She tied the other sleeve to a separate rung, allowing the shirt to hang like a banner. "That should do it." She gave a quick rattle to each of the bars, thinking if one of them was loose she could climb through, drop to the other side, and run for help. They didn't budge. "I'm coming down," she said as she climbed from Walter's shoulders to his thighs. She jumped to the ground and gently patted the wounded shoulder. "You're a better man than I," she said with a grin.

He smiled. "Well, I can't argue that...at least from the gender aspect."

Maddi slid into her shoes, picked up her scarf, and was about to tie it around Walter's wounded shoulder, when he waved her off. "I don't need it, Maddi."

He was right; the scarf had been a tourniquet to stop the bleeding. But now he was without a shirt, and it was cold in the dungeon. She walked over and grabbed his jacket from Henderson's legs and tossed it to him. He was about to object, when she shook her head. "Take it, Walter; it's freezing in here." She took off her sweater, leaving her with just her shirt. She laid the sweater over Henderson's legs, then wrapped the scarf around her like a cape. She sat and pulled Henderson's head onto her lap. She looked down to see him chuckling. "What's so funny?"

In a hoarse whisper, he said, "*Nani gigantum humeris insidentes.*"

Maddi pretended to glare at him.

He laughed. "Dwarfs standing on the shoulders of giants."

"I know what it means," she said, feigning anger. She bent down and kissed his forehead. "And it's true." She grinned, adding, "*Si vos cannot operor valde res, operor vegrandis res in a valde via.*"

Henderson's blue eyes gleamed as he looked at her and smiled sadly. "Ah yes. *If you cannot do great things, do small things in a great way.*" He pulled her closer and whispered, "Everything you do is great...there is nothing small about you."

CHAPTER 24

Outside Uzava, Latvia

"The goal is to send a message...and to start a war."

Those were the words that had been said to Vladimir Karev – *Zebulun* – by his father, Jacob. *"I will do as you ask, Father,"* he had replied without hesitation.

The night was bitter cold and he zipped his jacket to his chin as he wrapped a black wool scarf around his neck. He glanced at his watch: *11:00 p.m.* He had arrived at the Henderson compound thirty minutes ago, hitching a ride with a trucker from Riga on his way to Ventspils. He had had the driver drop him at Uzava just before he headed north. Keeping low to the ground, and using trees and underbrush for cover, he had reached the outer perimeter of the Henderson estate at 10:30. He had staked out a spot half-a-mile away so he could get a sense of the estate's security measures.

The compound was completely hidden; no lights, no entryway, no overhead wires to indicate that there was anything beyond the thick row of trees that sat a hundred feet from the road. But Zebulun knew what was there. He had studied closely the maps that Jacob had sent him in the email. He was aware of the compound that lay buried among the trees with the most sophisticated security money could buy. Jacob had said, *"It is the toughest you will find."* Zebulun wasn't concerned; he welcomed the challenge. *I come from Siberia, where every day is tough.*

He waited for clouds to cover the moon, then crossed to a spot directly across from the estate, in a field of tall winter wheat. Though cameras likely surveyed the area outside the compound, he doubted they were as diligent toward the field across the road. Even if they were, he felt confident in his ability to evade them by staying low and moving only when necessary. When he did move, it was with the wind, and the acute mindfulness that a simple snap of a wheat frond could mark his bitter end.

He was still wearing the dark jeans and black sweatshirt he had put on when he left Estonia, and his hair was still hidden under the beret that had belonged to his father, Viktor. As he settled in, with his belly to the ground, he thought of Viktor and the many missions his pilot father had completed on behalf of Russia. *All for nothing,* he thought with an acrid taste in his mouth. *But now I fight the right war.*

From inside his backpack, he pulled out night-vision goggles, along with his disassembled rifle. He put it together, then grabbed the two seven-inch Ka-bar knives from his coat pocket. They had been designed exclusively for killing. He had trained a lifetime for what he was about to do, thinking his efforts would be against Putin, never imagining that he would instead be fighting the entire world. No matter; his enemy wasn't important, only his triumph. He was uniquely skilled, having hunted in the Siberian wilderness most of his life. And, though he had mainly slain wolves or black bears, he had on occasion taken out an unwanted visitor who had surprised him in the backwoods. He smiled as he recalled Jacob asking about his skills. *"Do I need to provide you training, my son?"* Zebulun had laughed. *"No, father, I kill well."*

The moon crept from behind a cloud, bathing the knives in bright light. He quickly covered them with his coat. He felt affection for the knives; they were far more personal than a gun. He knew no greater joy than taking a man's life with one quick stab to the jugular. There was something almost holy about being close enough to feel life leave...about knowing, were it not for him, that man – or woman – would still be breathing...about sensing a soul's desperate grasp of how precious those final breaths truly were. *I show my victims the worth of their lives...as they are dying.*

The moon retreated behind the clouds, returning Zebulun to the comfort of shadow. He settled deeper in the wheat, then used his binoculars to stare between the fronds at the trees across the road. He knew what was behind those trees; he knew *who* was behind those trees. Though he had no idea why the mysterious Emek must die, he was prepared to slay him, nonetheless. He had come on a mission; he had come to kill.

"The goal is to send a message...and to start a war."

CHAPTER 25

Paris, France

By the time Jenny arrived at the hospital, it was after ten p.m. She was jet-lagged and exhausted from worry for her son, but she fought it as she ran from the taxi through the hospital's front door. A receptionist stopped her, reluctant to give her Roger's room number, but gave in when she saw tears in the eyes of the woman who claimed to be his mother. With a thick French accent, the woman said softly, "I am a mother too, madam." She then whispered the room number. Jenny nodded her thanks and ran down the hall toward his room. *Keep it together, Jenny.* She reached the door and stopped, fearful of what she might find on the other side. She looked through a small window and saw Hank and a young lady she didn't recognize sitting on opposite sides of a hospital bed. She couldn't look at the man on the bed, so she focused on Hank, hoping to get a sense of Roger's condition from her ex-husband's face. Hank was clearly exhausted; never had she seen him look so tired. He hadn't shaved, his hair was a mess, and there were dark circles under his eyes. It made him look old, and her heart ached for him. She was overwhelmed by a desire to rush in and comfort him. *Get a grip, Jenny.* She looked at the attractive young girl who sat on the other side of the bed. She was holding Roger's hand devotedly. *Who is she?* Jenny could almost feel the girl's heartache as she stared at Roger. Jenny slowly, reluctantly turned her own eyes to the bed. She gasped and covered her mouth as she saw her beautiful boy lying with IV's and tubes coming from every part of him. She wanted to see his eyes, his smile, but there was nothing. He just laid there, muffled hums from inert machines the only evidence that he was even alive. She held her breath and pushed open the door. Both Hank and the girl turned to look at her. Hank stood, a weak grin softening his features, though his eyes remained sad. She walked over to him and he hugged her. Roger's injuries were *not* mild; she could tell by the way Hank was holding her. His chin rested – like it used to – on top of her head, and she hugged him back, more tightly than she intended. It felt good to be embraced by this man who loved her son as much as she did. After a minute, she took a step back, wiping tears from her cheeks. "How is he?"

"He's okay. He's out of danger."

"Out of danger?" Jenny's voice was shaking. "Y—you told me it was minor."

Hank sighed. "I lied. I didn't want you flying across the ocean thinking the worst." He led her to a chair next to his. They sat solemnly, both staring at the unmoving figure lying in the bed. She was about to challenge Hank about the lie, when he pointed to the young woman and said, "This is Tonna Kauffold. She's a...friend of Roger's. Tonna, this is Roger's mother, Jenny."

Tonna smiled, her eyes gleaming as she extended a hand. "So nice to meet you, Mrs. Clarkson."

The British accent took her by surprise. She took Tonna's hand and squeezed it. "Please, call me Jenny. It's nice to meet you, as well."

Jenny stood and leaned close to Roger's ear. She whispered, "Your mother's here, baby," and put her hand to his cheek. She had been comforted by Hank's words: *"He's out of danger."* But was he? Would he ever be? *No...he's a CIA agent.*

As moonlight filtered into the room, the three of them kept a vigil by his bed. Jenny occasionally looked over at Tonna, trying to figure out the relationship between the girl and her son. It wasn't hard. *She's in love with him.* Such a strange thing...to see another woman loving her son. Roger had had girlfriends, but Jenny had never sensed anything deep with any of them. This felt different, but she didn't have Roger's reaction to gauge. She watched the young woman who sat faithfully at her son's side. She was lovely. The moonlight lit up her face, as if welcoming her as an equal to the gentleness of nighttime. Whoever she was, she possessed a tender soul, and Jenny could only pray that her kindness had made its way into Roger's subconscious.

Hank had leaned back in his chair and his eyes were closed; he was fighting sleep...it was clear that he had done the same thing many times in that chair. Jenny watched him, suddenly loving him the way she used to. She longed to lay next to him as they weathered yet another crisis in their stormy lives. Even with his eyes closed, Jenny could see his anguish, and she wanted to ask, *"What happened to Roger that has left you so tortured, dear Hank?"* She tried to imagine what he might say, the things he would tell her that had been done to their son. As the moon crossed the night sky, its soft light coursing its way into the room, she shook her head and sighed. *I don't ever want to know.*

CHAPTER 26

London, England

The plane landed at the London Airport at 10:40 p.m. Tall, lean Gustav Klein walked to the front of the terminal with his travel bag over one shoulder. He stopped in a bathroom and splashed water on his face, admiring himself in the mirror. His dark beard and mustache were perfectly groomed, and he wore a pair of black-rimmed glasses with a slight tint to the lenses. His hair was brown with hints of gray, and he wore it medium length, just below his ears. He pushed back a loose strand as he adjusted his tie and smoothed his collar; he was about to meet the Chief Inspector of Scotland Yard...it was important that he look respectable.

He walked outside and stood in line for a cab. It didn't take long. "Euston station, please," he said as he slid in back. The driver nodded and they pulled away. As they neared the city, he looked with mixed feelings at the sights and sounds of London. Though he was familiar with London, he had been gone for what seemed like a very long time; it felt good to be back. He wished he could visit a few of his favorite haunts. He shook his head and sighed. *Another time, perhaps.*

They reached the terminal and the driver stopped the car. "Euston, sir."

Klein paid the fare and got out of the cab. He walked into the station, picked up his ticket for the overnight train, then hurried to the back of the terminal. He spotted the train on track ten, and recognized the well-known inspector standing at the foot of a stairway, waiting to board. Klein gave him a wave and ran to meet him.

Pritchard, a small man with a hearty smile, stuck out his hand. "Dr. Klein, I presume?"

Klein shook the hand enthusiastically. "Yes. Good evening, Inspector. Thank you for taking time to see me. I'm looking forward to our trip to Edinburgh. The train will be a nice change of pace. Quite conducive to conversation, I'm sure."

Pritchard nodded, his thin mustache twitching as he said, "Yes, I agree."

He led the way up the steps and down a narrow corridor to their cabins. "I had the attendant secure you a compartment directly across from mine, Professor. If you'd like to unpack your things, I've arranged for coffee and brandy, then we can talk."

Klein nodded as he stepped into the charming, yet cramped quarters of the overnight train. He hadn't travelled in a sleeper car in years; he was looking forward to it. He unpacked his bag and organized his few items in the overhead carriage. He felt a sudden jolt as the train left the station and, once it was underway, he walked across to Pritchard's compartment. "Are you ready for me, sir?"

"Yes, have a seat, Professor."

Klein sat across from him and helped himself to a cup of coffee. He poured in a bit of the brandy, stirred it, then set the spoon on his plate, positioning it carefully so it wouldn't rattle when he lifted the cup. He took a sip of the coffee, then lowered the cup to the plate with a nod and a sigh. "Ah, excellent."

Pritchard smiled. "I hope your trip from Brussels was pleasant?"

"Yes, quite...thank-you."

"Good." He lowered his voice. "Now why don't you fill me in on what you know about," he leaned in and whispered, "...Cobra."

Klein tugged at his beard as he looked somberly at the inspector. Keeping his voice low, he said, "Let me start by saying that Dr. James Samuels is one of the finest psychiatrists I've had the pleasure to work with in my many years at the University."

Pritchard shrugged. "I'm not familiar with him, I'm afraid. He had tried to call me several times over the weekend, but I was out of town."

Klein frowned. "Interesting. Do you know what it was concerning?"

"No, he left only his name and number, and I've been unable to reach him."

"I see. I would guess it has something to do with what I'm about to tell you."

Pritchard leaned even closer. "I'm all ears, Klein."

Klein took another sip of coffee. "As I said, I got the call from Samuels," he paused, "...and he suggested that he might have a way to find Cobra."

"So, Samuels knows where he is?"

"I'm not sure if he knows just yet, but he's confident he'll know by morning."

"By morning? How odd."

"He also told me he wouldn't reveal Cobra's location; at least not right away."

"What? Why, I'll have the man arrested for obstruction. If he knows where the killer is, then he must tell me!"

"Yes sir, and I think he has every intention of doing so...eventually. But before he tells you where Cobra is hiding, he wants assurances."

"*Assurances?* Like what, for Pete's sake!" Pritchard's mustache was twitching. He cleared his throat, and lowered his voice even further. "Cobra is a cold-blooded murderer; surely that is the only *assurance* the man needs."

Klein nodded. "Yes, but as his doctor, Samuels holds a peculiar...fondness for the man. He'd like for you to come to him so the two of you can take Cobra...*alive.*"

"Wait a minute, Klein. You're telling me that Samuels is Cobra's *doctor?* How on earth—?"

"I believe that he took on that role just before Cobra...left town."

Pritchard shook his head. "No wonder he tried to call me." He sipped his coffee. "Fine. It's a bit irregular, but if he can help us find Cobra, then I'm willing to do whatever he asks...within reason. I can gather together several men and—"

"Alone ...no other officers."

The cabin grew silent. Pritchard frowned. "Alone? Why alone?"

"I'm not sure, Inspector. But he promised me that you would be safe."

Pritchard frowned. "I'm not worried about my safety; it's just that the man's an escape artist as well as a killer. One officer may not be enough," he smoothed his lapels, "...even if it is the Chief Inspector of Scotland Yard." He peered over his glasses. "What *assurances* can you give me that Samuels is trustworthy?"

Klein stared at Pritchard, his eyes nearly hidden by the tinted glasses as he stroked his beard thoughtfully. He reached into his pocket and pulled out a clear plastic bag which held an item about two inches wide. He set it in front of Pritchard, smoothing the edges so the item would show through. Pritchard pulled a magnifying glass from a chain around his neck and studied the item. "Good god, man!"

Klein nodded.

"Where did you get this?"

"From Samuels. He sent it in last night's post. He said that Mark Justice – Cobra's *alter ego* – had given it to him. It had been his first indication that they were one and the same...Justice and Cobra, I mean."

Pritchard's jaw dropped. "Mark Justice? One and the same? What the—"

"Dissociative Identity Disorder, it's called. 'Split personality' to the layman."

Pritchard had broken out in a sweat; he was clearly struggling with the news.

"Are you okay, Inspector?"

The older man cleared his throat. "I'm...I'm fine." But it was obvious that he wasn't. Sweat coated his brow, and he was tugging at his collar, seemingly having trouble getting a breath. He looked at Klein, and, with a tremor to his voice, he said, "Of...of all the cockamamy things I've been told on this job, that one takes the cake."

Klein flinched. "From what Samuels told me, I can vouch that it's the truth." He watched Pritchard as he stared at the name tag. Though it was still inside the plastic, the words – and the blood stains – were undeniable. That tag had belonged to Cora Winslow, the paramedic that Cobra had killed after he had left the Queen's Ball.

Pritchard's hands were shaking, and Klein was beginning to worry about the older man. "If you'd like, sir, I can call Samuels and say that you're unable to come."

Pritchard looked up from the nametag and stared at Klein with eyes that were terrifying in their intensity. With his voice a bit less shaky, he said, "I would sell my soul to find that...monster." He added, "You obtain information on his whereabouts, Klein. We will leave the minute I can get away from tomorrow's conference."

CHAPTER 27

On the train to Edinburgh, Scotland

It can't be! Pritchard thought, as he tried not to look at the nametag. He went to take a sip of his coffee, but his hand was shaking, and he was forced to set the cup in its saucer. He was completely undone by what he had just learned. He needed a minute to process it. *Justice is...Cobra!* He thought of all the things he had told Justice; all the times he had confided in the investigator as they had pursued killers in the realm, the most notable being Cobra, himself. He felt like he might be sick. He tried to look away, but couldn't turn his eyes from the blood-stained nametag. Of all the items he expected to see, Cora Winslow's nametag wasn't one of them. He was horrified, not only by what it represented, but by the thought of it passing through so many hands. First to Cobra, taken from the girl as he cut her to shreds; then to Justice, who had apparently – if Klein was to be believed – had it simply because of his dual identity with Cobra. It had then been given to Samuels as a symbol of Justice's battle with his newfound truth; and, finally – again, if Klein was to be believed – Samuels had sent it to Klein to ready him for a rendezvous the following day. Poor Cora's blood-soaked tag had traveled many a mile on its tour of carnage, but as he looked at it now, he felt an odd sense of respect for its journey...its stubborn tenacity...its voice from the grave. *Like Poe's 'Tell-Tale Heart,'* Pritchard thought. *"Dissemble no more! I admit the deed!"*

He thought back to the Cobra crimes that Justice had helped him solve. The sleuth had always seemed to have a second sense about the killer...*as if he knew him from the inside out.* He trembled as he checked his phone, likely for the fifteenth time. He had left a message for Samuels, and was now quite eager to get that return call. Was Klein telling the truth? If so, then Samuels would certainly be able to confirm it.

He swallowed, forcing an air of calm. "Tell me, Professor, how much do you know about Justice?"

Klein shook his head. "Not much. Only that if what Samuels says is true, Justice is an alter-ego to Cobra." He paused. "Which is quite remarkable, if you think about it. The condition is so rare."

Pritchard narrowed his eyes. "And how again do you know Samuels?"

Klein chuckled and looked out the window. "As I said, he was, at one time, my professor." His Austrian accent was thick. "Even then, the man was odd. His coursework was unique, a bit controversial, if you will." Klein looked at Pritchard, his eyes hard to read behind the dark glasses. "Samuels had insisted on referencing Freud as much as he could, even though by that time Freud's teachings had pretty much been discounted."

Pritchard frowned. "Why was that, do you suppose?"

Klein sighed. "I don't know. I can tell you that he was obsessed with going back...to the beginning." He flinched, again looking out the window, a million miles away. Pritchard watched him, curious what was going on in his psychoanalytic mind.

After a minute, Klein turned to Pritchard and sighed. "I wish we had all shared his interest in a man – or a woman's – past. I know now that that sort of psychotherapy can be quite illuminating."

Pritchard nodded, though he could hardly imagine how listening to someone dwell on their past while sprawled across a couch could be illuminating. He was intrigued by the man in front of him, however. His eyes, though barely visible behind the tinted lenses, seemed to look past Pritchard to another place, a different time...as if he was mired in his own journey. Pritchard recalled an article he had once read: *"A Psychiatrist's career is devoted to curing himself."* Was that the case here? He sat back and sighed. *And why is the man still wearing his sunglasses? The sun set hours ago.* He stared at the dark lenses. Were they prescription, perhaps?

He was about to ask, when Klein stood abruptly and stretched his arms. "You must forgive me, Inspector. The day has been a long one. I need to sleep."

Pritchard stood and shook the man's hand. "Certainly, Professor." He watched as the tall man bent his head to avoid hitting the jam of the cabin door. "Goodnight."

He watched him cross the hall into his own compartment. Pritchard grabbed his toiletries, stepping aside as the night porter came in to turn his room into a bedroom. He walked to the bathroom, readied himself for the night, and walked back to his room. He was looking forward to sleeping on the train. He and Klein were in agreement; there was nothing more conducive to conversation – or sleep – than the rhythmic back and forth of the train.

But first he needed to call the Yard. If what Klein had said was true, then sometime tomorrow, Pritchard would be in a position to confront Cobra. But Klein had been adamant that he couldn't pull in his team of officers. Samuels had insisted that Pritchard come alone. *If that's what it takes to finally come face-to-face with that butcher, then so be it.* He pulled out his phone and dialed. The Yard's night officer picked up the phone after the first ring. "Scotland Yard."

"Ethan, it's Pritchard. As you know, I'm heading up to Edinburgh on behalf of the Prime Minister. I'm guessing that will take much of the day tomorrow. After that, I'm going to need about twenty-for hours to take care of a bit of...personal business."

There was a pause. "Uh...yes sir."

"Don't make too much of it, Ethan, just a private matter that I must address. I may get back even sooner. I'll call in when I've handled the matter."

"Yes sir." Another pause. "Good luck, sir."

Pritchard ended the call and was about to plug his phone into his charger, when he decided to try Samuels one more time. He dialed the number, then cursed under his breath as it went to voicemail. He left no message, plugged his phone in the charger, then crawled under the sheets. He reached up and turned off a lamp by the bed. He looked out the window as the night sped by, thankful for the half-moon which cast a soothing light not only to the moors and waterways, but to his chamber, as well. He prayed that he would dream well...that the images in his sleep would be comforting. But he knew they wouldn't be; they hadn't been since the Queen's Ball.

As his eyelids grew heavy and the train trolled on with its gentle cadence, he drifted to sleep. But it wasn't the moon or the moors that he saw in his mind's eye. No, like every dream he had had for the last seven nights, all he could see was the beautiful Jane Harper dying in his arms.

CHAPTER 28

Somewhere over Europe

Dora Henderson was tired. No, she was more than tired...she was exhausted...spent...wiped out. And not only because of the hours-long journey across the Atlantic. She was tired because of all the battles she had been forced to fight...forever, it seemed. Her husband's affair; the death of her only child; the sham that had become her marriage with the magnificent Walter Henderson.

She sighed as she put a hand to her hair, golden blonde with the occasional streak of gray...*for authenticity*. After all, she was seventy-one now; it would be foolish for her to pretend that she was still young. She combed her fingers through it, adjusting an errant strand as if it mattered, smiling sadly as she thought about her husband in the quiet darkness of the plane. Walter truly was magnificent; in nearly every way. He was kind and commanding, smart and thoughtful, loving and wise. It was what had made the last thirty years of their fifty years together so difficult. She loved him...desperately...but she hated him, too. Thirty years. To think she had lived such a life...such a lie...for so long.

"Time waits for no man." She chuckled. *Or woman.* It was true. Somehow, in the blink of an eye, she had become old. Walter, too, though neither one looked like it. That was what came with money and access; the ability to push back time, at least a little. *But only on the outside,* she thought, as she stretched her legs to keep them from cramping. *In the end, time...and death...take us all.*

She replayed Walter's words in her mind. *"Martin is...alive, okay?"* The words had stunned her. How could it be? She and Walter had buried Martin – or at least his memory –

on a hillside outside DC. But Walter had been adamant. *"I have it on good authority that he's alive...alright?"* Her first thought had been, *I won't believe it...I can't.* But she knew that Walter wouldn't say it if it wasn't true. The man wasn't above lying to her, but he would never lie about something like that.

Would he?

She checked her watch. *One a.m. in France.* Which meant that it was seven p.m. back home. She didn't mind being in the plane at that hour. After all, if she was home in their Boston mansion, she would be seated at the oversized table in the grand dining room eating an elegant dinner...alone. There would be a fire, the chandelier would be on low light; it would be a beautiful setting. But that beauty would only heighten her loneliness. It wasn't that Walter never dined with her. When he was in Boston, he ate breakfast and dinner with Dora. The problem was that he was rarely in Boston. And, most of the time, he was away for the right reasons.

She had thought about taking a lover, but the whim had drifted through her mind like a feather on a breeze. It hadn't made it even close to her heart. Dora didn't ache for a man; she ached for Walter.

On occasion, she would ask dear, devoted Kate to join her for dinner, and – though in the beginning, her aide of over forty years had resisted – she had finally conceded to a seat at the table and half a glass of wine. Kate seemed to understand that women like Dora didn't have friends in the way that most people did. Her life was public, yet private, full, yet empty, enviable, yet sad. Kate seemed to grasp it better than most, as a matter of fact, and had willingly taken on the mantle of trust. But she would excuse herself before the main course, the norms of aides and overseers drilled into her over years of having served. Dora had begun to accept that most of her meals would either be with a roomful of supplicants, or spent alone by the fire, with little more than a second glass of wine to keep her company.

She loved Walter, and she knew that he loved her, too. But it wasn't that simple. She closed her eyes and thought of all the twists and turns that had led her to where she was...on a private jet, flying to meet her estranged yet esteemed husband, who had just told her that their dead son was alive. If it wasn't so tragic, it would be laughable. *To think...little Dora McGregor's life has come to this.*

Born in Scotland in 1933, Dora Jane Mary McGregor had grown up never imagining that she would wed the heir not only to a vast fortune, but to a globally-recognized name. But with that role had come responsibility...and a lot of pain. Not just from Walter's deception; she had come to accept that in due course. But from the people who were reliant on her unspoken obedience to rules it had taken her years to learn. What she had finally understood was that her role was one of continuity and devotion to a deity she couldn't quite identify. She needed to always be the faithful wife, the dutiful public servant, the tireless mother. If she faltered in any way, then those relying on her prostration to that unnamed deity would fail, as well. In some ways, it reminded her of stories she had read of the British aristocracy. She hadn't lived in Scotland long enough to acquire an insider's glimpse into the royal family, but she had seen enough to know that the symbols of the monarchy were far more important than any tiresome truths. She, too, had learned to live up to a similar sort of symbolism. And, much like the monarchy, she had no idea what would happen should she fail. All she knew was that she couldn't.

She had been raised to never complain, so she didn't; or at least not loudly, even when three pregnancies left her with only one child, or when her husband chose to bed another woman, or when her only child was killed in a DC hotel ballroom. No, Dora had taken it all in stride, with the charm and grace that had been inspired by her mother, and insisted upon by her grandmother, who – according to her uncle – was a distant relative to a distant queen. It was a lot to live up to, and Dora had done her best...both for her grandmother and for her husband.

She looked out again at the sky. Clouds covered the moon, and the darkness was nearly complete. It seemed fitting...a vacuum waiting to be filled. She had packed hurriedly once she had gotten Walter's call, unsure how long she would be gone. She and Kate had been driven to the airfield, whisked through security, and directed to the Henderson private plane, where Gerald was standing by, ready and waiting. Now, seven hours later, here she was, hovering over France, about to see her dead son who was allegedly alive. They were expected to land in Lyon soon, and, though she had sat calmly while the Citation X cruised at 600 miles per hour, inside she was a quivering mess. If it was true – if Martin was alive – then suddenly none of the other disappointments of her life seemed important. So what if Walter had a mistress; many well-to-do men had mistresses. She knew he loved her, and could almost forgive him for his indiscretions...*if Martin is alive*. It was like a bargain with God: *"I vow to never find fault with my circumstances or regret the turn of events in my life if you give me back my son."*

She tried to imagine what Martin might look like after suffering through the fire. He would be scarred, and his hair would likely be a far cry from the below-the-ears cut that had so characterized his carefree spirit for so long. Was he still carefree? How could he be after enduring such an ordeal. But more than his looks, or even his countenance, the question that was haunting her most was his silence. Why on earth wouldn't he tell her? Why wouldn't her beloved son let her –

his mother – know that he – *her only son* – was alive? Was it because he was no longer handsome? Surely, he knew that a mother didn't care...that a mother thought her child was handsome, regardless. Was it because he was ashamed? *Of what?* came the quick reply. What on earth would Martin have to be ashamed of. Honestly, if it wasn't Walter who was telling her that Martin was alive, she would never believe it...because of his silence.

She thought of her own life. She had had things to be ashamed of...plenty of them, but she had never hidden from them...had she? Though her relationship with her husband hadn't turned out how she might have wanted, she had never felt compelled to hide it. She flinched. *Sure you did, Dora.* Her society friends didn't know about Walter's girlfriend in the Philippines; she had managed to keep the entire affair secret for almost thirty years. Why? *For appearances.* Once again, the importance of symbolism. As if they were the king and queen of Boston, Walter and Dora attended the balls, the ballets, the benefits...arm-in-arm, as if nothing could ever come between them. If she could hide in that charade for thirty-odd years, then surely Martin could hide for a mere four. But why would he? *What has he got to hide?*

She felt a sudden drop in altitude and clung tightly to her purse. She looked over at Kate, who nodded reassuringly. The aide had been at Dora's side through every major hardship; miscarriages, Walter's affair, Martin's death, and the many soulless nights when Walter had left her alone. Dora valued Kate's friendship every bit as much as she appreciated her loyalty. The woman – tall, thin, and filled with the strength of one who had known her own share of hardship – had stood with her through it all; she had been a trusted confidant and a truly good friend. Dora caught her eye and smiled; Kate smiled back as the plane continued to descend. Dora loved Kate's smile. It was as if Kate had invented the notion of unconditional love, and it was exemplified by that simple, timeless smile.

They hit the tarmac and Dora was pushed against the seat. She clung to the arms of her chair as the jet slowed and cruised to the terminal. She suddenly felt lightheaded. She closed her eyes and took long, slow breaths. If Walter was telling the truth, then she was about to see her son...for the first time in four very long, very lonely years.

She went to grab her carryon, but Kate beat her to it, reaching across the aisle and lifting it by the strap. The devoted aide nodded and smiled. "I've got it, Dora."

Dora nodded in reply. Kate had her bag...and her back. As a result, Dora was ready. With Kate as her armor, and a mother's love as her shield, she would meet her husband and hopefully see her son. But she would wait to believe it. *My boy stays buried...until I see him face-to-face.*

Chapter 29

Lyon, France

Andrew Madison checked his watch. *One a.m....let's go!* He had been on the train from Paris for a full two hours, and he was growing impatient. He leaned back in the seat, closing his eyes in an effort to fall asleep. But he couldn't sleep. Maddi was missing, and her agents had been killed. It was a horrific turn of events, and had left him broken inside. The minute he had grasped what had happened, he had stormed out of the de Crillon meeting room and had run down three flights of stairs to the lobby. Kauffold had followed him in the elevator, and had caught up to him as he was waiting for a cab. Kauffold had tried to convince him to stay in Paris, and to leave Maddi's disappearance to the authorities. It hadn't worked. *"They don't know her like I do,"* Andrew had told him.

The only information he had was that Maddi had last been seen in a public square in Lyon. Unfamiliar with France and having no one to ask, he had had the cabby drive him to the nearest train station. He had booked a train to Lyon, but unfortunately, the only train with an open seat didn't leave until eleven p.m., which wouldn't get him to Lyon until one-thirty in the morning. He had thought about renting a car, but Lyon was five hours away by car. The late train would be quicker.

He had spent the time looking through maps of Lyon, trying to familiarize himself with the city. But with no point of reference, it had been of little help.

He stretched his legs and tried to get comfortable as he did his best to not think about Maddi...who might have her, what he might be doing to her. Whoever he was, he had killed one agent and wounded another; he clearly wasn't averse to killing.

After another twenty minutes, the train reached Lyon. Andrew left the train and waited for a taxi outside the station. A cab pulled up and Andrew slid in back. "The town square."

"Place Bellecour?"

"Yeah, sure." They reached the square in twelve minutes, and it was instantly clear that it was a crime scene. Even at two in the morning, there was a lot of activity; police, private investigators, forensics officers with their high-density lights and their low-density conversations. A few gawkers had gathered nearby, as well.

Andrew got out of the cab, paid the fare, and ran to the square. He stopped about ten feet away from two police officers who were standing in front of an area roped off with crime scene tape. Andrew swallowed uncomfortably as he noted several different chalk marks in the shapes of bodies etched on the ground behind them. He walked up to one of the officers. "What...what happened here?"

The officer frowned. In French, he said, "None of your business, *American.*"

Unmoved by the insult, Andrew nodded. "What if I told you I know one of the victims," he said, hoping that would cause them to adopt a different tone. It didn't.

The officer said derisively, "Yes, that is right. You and every other nosy person willing to stand here at two in the morning. Go away, American tourist."

Andrew walked over to a couple of bystanders about a hundred yards away. "So, do you guys know what happened?"

Fortunately, one of them spoke English. "At least six people dead, two others led away, they think by whoever was responsible."

"Do you know who the two were that were led away?"

"No one is saying. As a matter of fact, they are saying little about any of it."

Andrew spent another hour walking the square, looking for clues to tell him where Maddi might have been taken. Finally, with nothing but aching feet and a very tired body, he looked around and sighed. *Where are you, Maddi?* No one seemed to know anything, or if they did, they weren't willing to share.

He yawned and rubbed his eyes. He needed sleep. He hadn't slept hardly at all since his flight from America two nights ago. But he couldn't leave the square, not until he had some idea what had happened to his sister. If only he could talk to someone who had been there. *If only Maddi's agents were alive and could tell me what happened.*

Suddenly he stopped. His eyes widened. *What about Seacroft?* From what Kauffold had told him, the man had been injured, but not killed. Had Seacroft maybe seen something that might help Andrew find Maddi? The agent would certainly have more to offer than the officers in the square. Again, he yawned, and again, he rubbed his eyes. He could barely walk. He needed sleep. *I'll find a place to rest...and then I'll find Seacroft.*

Chapter 30

Uzava, Latvia...Erkner, Germany

Zebulun checked his watch. It was nearly two a.m. He had been hiding in the weeds for hours; he was getting restless. He reached again for his thermal night goggles and looked between wheat fronds and through a gap between the trees that fronted the Henderson estate. The trees, which were still without foliage, moved with the wind, allowing him to see slivers of the compound...the flicker of a light here and there; the reflection from the full moon on an unnoticed bit of metal. Together, those flickers and reflections created an image in his mind; a way to visualize a compound that had been effectively hidden from the world. He scanned back and forth, as he had done for the past three hours, just waiting for his opportunity.

Jacob had told him little about the soldiers that protected the compound, other than to say that they had a duty to protect not only the Henderson estate, but the country of Latvia, as well, and were therefore well-armed. He had also said that there were fewer than usual. He hadn't said why; it didn't matter. Zebulun would take advantage of it.

He was waiting for them to take a break; even soldiers need a break, especially on a bitter cold night along the coast of Latvia. And it was irrefutably cold; well below zero, he was certain. But it wasn't a problem; Zebulun was from Siberia. He knew how to handle the cold. Dressed in layers of neoprene, and wearing a hooded parka, he had wrapped a black wool scarf over his mouth and nose. His gloves were made of leather Gore-Tex, and he wore Yak's wool socks inside his boots. The only part of him not covered were his eyes.

He looked again through the night goggles. For the first time since he had begun watching the compound, he saw movement; the guards were changing shifts. Still, he waited. How many guards were there? He didn't know, but he guessed that even at two a.m. a complex such as the Hendersons would be guarded by thirty men, no less. And it was likely that there was also an army within the walls of the estate.

But Zebulun wasn't there to take out an army. All he cared about was one man; one soldier who had taken center stage; one captain about whom Jacob had been very specific. *"You must kill Emek, my son. He is the man in charge of security."*

Zebulun had done all he could to learn about Emek; to get inside his head. Jacob had told him all that he knew of the man; Zebulun had used his own insight to figure out the rest. The man in charge of such a place would feel a heavy burden. He would sleep only a few hours at a time, and would spend most of his days – and nights – in the security room, overseeing the men. *It is what I would do.* He would be hesitant to leave the castle...ever, for fear of shirking his responsibility. But Zebulun couldn't go inside the castle to kill him; it would be suicidal. So, he would need to create a disruption that would be big enough to force Emek to leave that room and that castle, and venture outside. *Then I will kill him.*

He looked again through his night goggles. Though he was only able to see flashes of light, he had learned through many years of hunting bear in Siberia how to detect the movement of his prey without having to see the animal...or the man. Flashes and flickers suggested men on the move, which meant that it was time.

He looked up, thankful for a row of thick clouds that had come out of nowhere to blacken the sky. He gathered his gear, then sprinted across the road, staying low as he ran to a row of trees that lined the southeast corner of the compound. He found a large rock, bordered on one side by a thick elm tree. He huddled between the rock and the tree. From there, with the aid of the night goggles, he was able to see a swath of ground beyond the gate. There were shadows from muted lampposts; their soft light would be helpful. He lowered the binoculars and picked up his rifle. Holding it to his shoulder and using the sight, he spotted one of the guards as he passed under a lamp. The man was dressed in body armor from head to toe, but Zebulun knew exactly where to hit him. There was a one-inch area between the helmet and the neck armor that was impossible to protect. But Zebulun would have to angle the shot perfectly. He waited as the man marched beneath the lamp and turned; Zebulun aimed and fired. The soldier fell to the ground. Zebulun saw a shadow move. He watched as a second guard ran to the fallen soldier, laid flat on the ground beside him, then reached over to feel for a pulse. The man spoke into a radio as he rolled toward the protective cover of a tree. Zebulun timed his shot, and hit that soldier in the same vulnerable place on his neck. The radio fell from his hand. The call must have gone through, however, because the next thing he saw was a drawbridge lowering at the end of the castle closest to him. Light from behind the barricade allowed him to see a river underneath the bridge. The river surrounded the castle like a moat. A dozen soldiers ran across, but before they could reach the end, Zebulun took a grenade from his pocket, pulled the pin, and hurled it at the soldiers. All twelve fell onto the bridge.

He had evened the odds, at least a little, and, with the light from inside the castle, he was able to see more of the compound. He turned his sight to the north, but saw no one. He looked back at the drawbridge, watching in awe as the bridge, only slightly damaged from the grenade, was hoisted in the air, dead soldiers falling from each side. *Like something from the Middle Ages.*

The moon broke through the clouds, and he raised his goggles to his eyes. *Where are you, Emek?* A well-trained captain wouldn't stay inside while his soldiers were being picked off several at a time; he would feel the need to help. Zebulun hoped so; otherwise, he would need to find a way into the castle. He had memorized Emek's features from Jacob's email. *"Your target is in his late forties. He's six-two, lean, quick and very capable...a seasoned soldier, my son. He will be dressed in black. His clothes, his hat, even his mustache; all black."*

Zebulun frowned. Even if Zebulun did appear outside the castle, he would be covered in armor. How would Zebulun know it was him? He shifted position. *I will know...I have been trained to know.*

Fortunately, Emek's features were distinct. Though Zebulun wouldn't be able to see the man's signature hat, he should be able to pick up his mustache, and assess his age. *Forty-year-old men look very different than the fresh-faced soldiers they command.*

More soldiers appeared, this time from the north end of the castle. Every one of them was dressed in full armor. Zebulun counted them; again, there were twelve. He waited, watching each man as he crept stealthily in Zebulun's direction. Sporadically, one of the men would raise a visor, then quickly lower it. Would the raising of that visor be enough to let him get a look at Emek? *I must force them to lift those visors more often, and for a longer period of time.*

He reached in his pack and pulled out three M-18 smoke grenades. He stuffed two in his pocket, and tossed the third directly into the team of soldiers. He waited. The smoke filled the air in front of him, his night goggles allowing him to see through the smoke. He watched as one after the other, the men pulled up their visors. He looked at each face. When he was sure that Emek wasn't among them, he reached in his pack, took out a shoulder-fired missile, and positioned it on his right shoulder. Again, he waited. In spite of the smoke, the soldiers were moving closer. He wasn't afraid; Zebulun was never afraid. As a matter of fact, he was void of any emotion. He narrowed his eyes and nodded. *I am a perfect killing machine.*

He heard the crackle of a twig about twenty feet away. He aimed the missile and fired. It exploded with a crack. The cries of soldiers shattered the silence. Zebulun looked through his goggles. From what he could tell, the blast had taken out all twelve. He spotted another brigade approaching from the north. There were only six men. He threw another smoke bomb. All six lifted their visors. Still no Emek. Zebulun positioned the missile and fired again. The blast lit up the night sky, and was accompanied by more cries from dying soldiers. He chuckled. *Twelve on the drawbridge; eighteen here. Thirty in all...shall I make it fifty?*

He needed to move. The blasts would make it easy for the guards to find him; he wasn't ready to be found; not by the guards, anyway. *It must be Emek who comes for me.*

He left the missile launch behind, tucked his rifle over his shoulder, and crept from his hiding spot. Staying low, he ran about a hundred yards along the perimeter, then dove into an arc of tall grass. He edged toward the estate and stopped at a break in the trees. He spotted a thick metal fence protecting the compound. Lying on his stomach, he crawled to the fence, put his gun to his shoulder, and looked between the bars. Still wearing his night goggles, he was able to see much of the compound, but he saw no more soldiers. Had they retreated? *Or are they just lying in wait?*

All at once, he spotted a dozen guards running from the front of the castle, fanning out across the estate. They hit the ground, rolled, then zigzagged to their spots. He pulled out another smoke bomb – his last – and tossed it toward the men. One by one, they lifted their visors. He searched their faces. No Emek. He began to shoot them...like target practice. Suddenly, from behind a tree, a tall, lanky man ran to the aid of one of the fallen men. In an act of kindness that defied not only the logic of the situation, but the sense of compassion that Zebulun had buried years ago, the man knelt beside the dying soldier and lifted the man's head onto his lap. He raised the dying soldier's visor as well as his own, and the moonlight fell on his face. Zebulun's heart began to race. *It is him...it is Emek.* Angled cheekbones and an etched brow were visible in the few seconds the visor was raised; the face of a soldier who had known too many battles – either fought or anticipated – over the years. His narrowed eyes reflected his grief as he locked eyes with the dying soldier. Zebulun increased his magnification. He was able to see a mustache moving up and down as Emek said a prayer, or perhaps a final goodbye. Zebulun swallowed, fighting an urge to respect him. He tightened his jaw. *Then again, who better to kill than a worthy foe?*

He raised his pistol, aimed at the man's neck and, without a moment's pause, he fired. As if he had seen it coming, Emek fell to the ground and rolled behind a tree, the bullet slipping past him with a crack as it hit the trunk of the tree. *Dammit!* Zebulun waited. *Come out, Emek.* Within seconds, the captain ran to another tree, then fired in Zebulun's direction. Zebulun jerked just in time; the bullet whizzed past him. He fired back, and, again, Emek seemed to anticipate it and was able to move out of the way. Zebulun waited. Suddenly, he saw Emek run like a black streak toward a grove of trees twenty feet closer to where Zebulun was hiding. Zebulun fired four quick shots, each one a half-step in front of the other. A cloud passed over the moon; Zebulun lost sight of his target. He scanned the area. To his delight, he spotted Emek lying on the ground, his hand clutching his neck as he tried to scoot to the grove of trees. Zebulun's heart felt as if it would burst, feelings of both pride and grief overwhelming him. But he wasn't done. He had been instructed to attach a message to the man's body. *Which means I will need to go in there and get him.*

He was about to search for a way in through the gate, when he was startled by an explosion. The earth around him shook as fire from the blast lit up the night sky and pieces of dirt flew everywhere. A projectile had been sent from somewhere in the compound. *They, too, have missiles...much bigger than mine!* He shoved his goggles in his pack, grabbed the pack and his rifle, and ran as fast as he could away from there. Another projectile hit the ground within inches of him. *Run, Zebulun!* With the pack over his shoulder and the rifle under his arm, he sprinted north, staying low, using the thick grass as cover. A third missile hit the ground just inches away, and he put a hand to his head – an imaginary helmet – as he ran to the northernmost corner of the compound. There was another blast...it hit the ground far too close to him. He spotted a ravine and, with the pack on his shoulder and still holding his rifle, he leapt over the side of the ravine. He reached for a tuft of grass with his free hand, unwilling to let go of the rifle. He lost his grip and slid, and was about to career all the way to the bottom, when his elbow hit against a tangled tree root about halfway down. He grabbed it with his free hand, but his feet had nowhere to go. They dangled in the air, and, as he tried to gain his footing, he could hear bits of gravel hitting the bottom of the ravine. He guessed it to be another thirty feet, at least. Still holding the rifle, he clung to the root, his foot finally finding a wedged-in rock. His heart was pounding; he was having trouble getting his breath. *Relax, Zebulun, you have done this a hundred times.* And he had...so many times, in his native Russia. He had jumped ravines and scaled cliffs to hunt...or be hunted. *This is no different.*

He looked around. The ravine, clearly a barrier to the north end of the estate, had a drop of well over fifty feet. The entire gorge was surrounded by a thick, impenetrable forest, and he guessed it was booby-trapped with mines. Which meant that his only way inside was to somehow get across that ravine.

He took a deep breath and slung the strap of his rifle over his shoulder along with his backpack. Using buried tree limbs and the rare, well-placed rock, he edged skillfully along the inner wall of the cliff. He was glad he was so far below the ridge; it gave him cover. He could hear soldiers' footsteps in the trees above, as well as the occasional blast from a handheld missile. The soldiers were close, but it was clear they had no idea he was in the ravine. He kept going, nearly falling to his death at least five times before reaching the other side of the ravine. *Now, to get to the top.* Digging his boot deep into the dirt, he reached for a tree root a few feet above him. He grasped it with gloved fingertips and pulled himself up. Roots were scarce, his legs were shaking, and the tips of his gloves were torn. But he kept on, inspired not only by the hopeful light of the moon, but by his need to please Jacob. After another five minutes, he reached the top and tossed his rifle and his pack over the ridge. He heaved himself up, grabbed the rifle and the backpack, and crawled to the shelter of a clump of trees. He found a hidden spot unseen by the moon, and laid on his back to catch his breath. He listened, but heard nothing; no footsteps, no whispers. He had done it; he had gotten inside the compound. Though it was tempting to simply kill a few soldiers and get out, Jacob had been clear: *"You must send a message, my son."*

With his pack once again on his back, and his rifle over his shoulder, he crawled toward where Emek had fallen.

Zebulun's mastery of landmarks was like no other. Using the triangular placement of lampposts, trees, and rocks, he knew how to find him. But it was slow going. One wrong move could snap a twig or rustle a leaf, and he would be shot dead. He stopped. He had heard whispers. He waited. *Soldiers, less than ten feet away.* He scanned the area. He spotted the lifeless Emek about ten feet in the opposite direction. He slid onto his belly and crept slowly through the brush. After several minutes, he reached Emek's body. He laid still. He still heard whispers, but they were moving away from him.

After another minute, he stood and grabbed Emek under the shoulders. Moving as stealthily as he could, he dragged him deeper into the trees. He waited. Whispers still echoed through the branches, and he could hear footsteps, but they were moving in the opposite direction. He hadn't been spotted...yet.

Out of nowhere came a groan. Zebulun tensed. He stared at Emek. The man wasn't dead! His mouth opened; he was about to moan again. Zebulun slapped his hand over Emek's mouth. With his free hand, he pulled a Ka-bar knife from his pocket and sliced the man's throat. The man arched; Zebulun's heart stopped. But there were no further sounds; Emek was dead. Zebulun wiped the knife on Emek's jacket and slid it in his pack. *Silenced by the knife...like so many before him.*

Zebulun held his breath. He didn't make a move for a full minute. Though he could hear soldiers' whispers, they were still moving away from him. He let out the breath quietly, then took another. In spite of the cold air, he was sweating. He wiped his forehead with his coat sleeve as he waited for his heart to slow. When he was ready, he grabbed Emek by the shoulders and began dragging him through the trees.

After several minutes of dragging and lifting and dragging some more, he reached the northwest perimeter, where he was stopped by a twelve-foot metal fence. There was barbed wire across the top, and electric wires visible throughout. He touched the fence lightly with his gloved hand. A spark went through him and he fell backward into the dirt. *Dammit!* Climbing the fence was out. He would either have to double back and face the Henderson artillery, or somehow figure a way past the fence. He rubbed his neck, then grudgingly pulled a trowel from his pack. He bent down and began digging at the base of the fence. He prayed that those who had built it hadn't gone deeper than the customary two feet with the posts or the electrical grid. He dug quickly and efficiently, every motion useful as he removed large amounts of dirt in only a few minutes. He wiped sweat from his forehead as he shoved aside the dirt and dug some more. When he had gone a foot below the expected two, he slowly extended his hand under the fence, holding his breath as he waited to see if he would trigger an alarm. He sighed with relief when, after three minutes, he had heard neither sirens nor the stomp of soldiers' boots. He put the trowel in his pack, shoved his rifle and his pack under the fence and over to the other side, then slid his small, agile body underneath. When he made it to the other side, he reached under the fence for Emek. He grabbed the man's collar and dragged him until he was able to grip him under his shoulders. He tugged hard, ready to pull him on through, when the man's jacket caught on a piece of fence. Zebulun reached under and tried to dislodge the jacket. He couldn't get to it. Finally, he stood and, grabbing Emek by his neck and chin, he tugged with all his might. He felt the tension give way as the jacket tore, his own legs buckled, and Emek's body fell on top of him. Zebulun flailed frantically to get out from under the dead man. He jumped to his feet, tore off his gloves, and wiped his shaking hands on his jacket. He rubbed his eyes and looked up; the clouds were again covering the moon. *Good.* The darkness centered him; it gave him strength. He put on his gloves, slung his backpack on one shoulder, his rifle on the other, then grabbed Emek by the arms and dragged him a hundred feet or so to a field of tall grass.

He still had to figure out how to leave a message on the body that the other soldiers would see. He looked around; there was nothing but an old barn about twenty feet away. Leaving Emek in the grass, he sprinted to the barn and cautiously looked inside. It was pitch black. He reached in his pack and pulled out a box of matches. He lit one and looked around. There wasn't much; the barn was mostly empty except for a rusted bucket and a pile of moldy hay. Suddenly, his light fell on a pitchfork, its prongs buried deep in the dirt. He grinned. *That will work.*

He blew out the match and yanked the pitchfork from the ground. He carried it back to Emek and laid it over top of him. He dragged the body east through the trees, staying as low as he could. Though he was outside the perimeter, he knew that a compound like theirs would have cameras spanning the area. He bent even lower, making sure to stay below the height of the grass. But it was hard to drag a man as heavy as Emek while bent in such a position; his back began to ache. He was relieved when he came to the ravine, which marked the front corner of the compound. He dragged the body around the north ledge on a path less than two feet wide.

When he finally reached the other side, he dropped to his knees in the tall grass. The road was just a few feet away. He waited. No footsteps, no whispers, no bullets; he hadn't been spotted. He gathered his strength, then lugged the body onto the road until it was directly in front of the entrance. He pulled out an envelope with a printed copy of Jacob's note inside, unlatched the dead man's armor, and laid the note on his chest. Zebulun stood over the body, raised the pitchfork and, as hard as he could, gouged it into the man's chest, making sure to trap the note with the prongs. *There is your message, Jacob.*

He took a quick look at his handiwork, gave a satisfied nod, then sprinted away from the estate. The moon was still behind the clouds, and he ran north in the darkness, using trees by the road for cover. Just when he had begun to relax, he heard shots in the distance. He tensed as he looked warily over his shoulder. Soldiers were on the road running after him. He could see their high-powered rifles. He ran faster.

Soon, he heard the sound of a car's engine behind him. He ran even faster. He spotted a sign that said "Uzava, three miles," and, using mental maps he had made from those in Jacob's email, he determined his location. There should be a rest stop about two miles ahead. The car was getting closer. He sprinted hard, zigzagging through the trees, reaching the stop in fifteen minutes. He stood in the parking lot, hands on his knees as he gulped in air. He heard an engine and looked over his shoulder. The black sedan was less than a hundred feet away. *Shit!* He ran into the trees and a bullet ricocheted just inches from his left foot. He ran faster, snaking his way through the forest. Another shot hit a rock in front of him. He swerved, dove through the brush, then rolled down a hill into a creek. He stood and looked up. He was surrounded by dozens of tall, thick elm trees. More shots. His clothes were wet and he was exhausted, but there was no time to rest. He continued on through the trees. He came to a grove of cedars and climbed the first one he saw, scaling it as if he was a squirrel. He found a perch between two branches, wedging his feet until he felt solid. He waited. An owl hooted in the distance, and the flutter of bats' wings could be heard overhead. He slowed his breathing as he took his rifle from over his shoulder. He reached in his pack for his night-vision goggles and his knives. He sat with the rifle in his lap, and the knives on the branch beside him. He had a clear view of the entrance to the trees, and, though it was pitch black, the darkness was an ally. He had become one with the shadows, just another ghost hiding in the night. He heard footsteps; they were coming. He waited. He saw four men hiking capably between the trees. Unlike the others, these soldiers didn't have on body armor. They were dressed instead in all black, with their faces painted black, as well. They looked like Ninja warriors from the 19th century, and moved like them, as well. *The Hendersons have brought out their most elite fighters.* He chuckled. *It will be their biggest mistake.*

He raised one of the knives, kissed the blade, then threw it at the first man. It hit him square in the forehead, splitting his skull between his eyes. The man slumped to the ground without a sound. Before the others could react, Zebulun did the same with the second knife, again piercing the forehead of an unsuspecting soldier. A third man threw a knife at Emek and hit him in his left arm. He winced as he checked the wound. *Barely a scratch.* He raised his rifle, waited for the man to reappear, then shot him in the chest. He watched the man fall to the ground. He removed the knife from his arm, pulled a bandana from his pack, and wrapped it over the wound, all the while scouting the trees for the fourth and final man. Zebulun spotted his shadow behind a tree. *Do you fear me, Ninja warrior?* He smiled. *Of course, you do.* He reached in his pack and pulled out a flare. He lit it and threw it in the brush near to where the man was hiding. The flare lit up the area like a floodlight. The man ran from his hiding place, staying low as he weaved through the trees. Zebulun laughed; it had been too easy. He held his gun to his shoulder and waited. The man ran behind an old elm and stopped. After nearly a minute, he looked out cautiously, and, in half-a-second, his brains were splattered on the tree. It was done. Zebulun had single-handedly taken out much of the Henderson army. But he knew there would be more.

He shimmied down the tree and ran back to the rest area. He was about to steal the Henderson car when he stopped. Two more sedans were pulling in. A team of soldiers jumped out, all with RPG bazookas on their shoulders. *Shit!* He sprinted back through the woods, covering the now-familiar terrain quickly as he leapt over stumps and debris. He reached the northernmost edge of the trees and stopped. He could hear footsteps and whispers not far behind. He looked past the tree line for a place to hide. He spotted a dirt road about a hundred feet beyond the trees, and ran in that direction, thankful again for the clouds still blocking the moon. He saw a single streetlamp on the other side of the road and ran toward it. As he got closer, he could see a house set back from the road. He looked around, finally spotting what he was looking for; an old pickup truck was parked in a driveway in front of the house. He crept to it and was about to open the driver side door, when a dog's bark shattered the silence. He flinched. The dog, a hefty mixed-breed weighing about 90 pounds, inched closer, his teeth bared, a low growl hissing from his throat. *Think, Zebulun!* Using slow, careful movements, he reached in his pack and grabbed two slabs of beef jerky. He threw the jerky on the ground. The dog sniffed it. Zebulun raised his rifle and held it steady. He didn't want to shoot a dog, not only because of his love for the creatures, but because the gunshot would reveal his position. But he would have no choice if the animal jumped him. The dog continued to sniff, his teeth still bared, another low growl filling the silence. Zebulun waited. Finally, the animal nuzzled the jerky, put both pieces in his mouth, and ran away. Zebulun breathed a sigh of relief as he opened the door of the truck. He was about to slide behind the wheel, when he heard a loud boom. He fell across the seat just as a projectile sped past the truck and exploded in a nearby shed. He reached under the dash, yanked out wires, and tied the appropriate two together.

The engine roared to life. He sat up and slammed the car into gear just as another explosive hit the ground, just inches from the truck. He backed out of the drive and spun onto the dirt road, dust flying everywhere. He shifted and sped east, another blast sending debris into the air directly behind him. There was a road up ahead that he knew would take him north to Kolka, a port on the Gulf of Riga, about forty miles away. He checked the gas gauge; less than a quarter tank. *It should get me close.*

He drove at top speed, continually checking his mirrors, heartened when he saw that there was no one behind him. Had he done it? Had he lost them? He didn't dare relax, or enjoy the quiet. *Not until I get to that plane.*

He ran out of gas about two miles from Kolka. He grabbed his backpack and his rifle, climbed out, and shifted the truck into neutral. He gave it a heave from behind, watching with satisfaction as it crept to the edge of a cliff, slipped over the side, and fell into the ravine. The sounds of crumbling metal and breaking glass shattered the silence, but from what he could tell, there was no one to hear it but him. He pulled his pack over his shoulders, slid his rifle under his arm, and ran to Kolka, using the trees along the side of the road for cover. He stopped now and then to catch his breath and listen for cars; still nothing. He had nearly reached Kolka when he stopped. He could hear engines overhead. *Shit! The Hendersons have helicopters!*

He sprinted the final hundred yards, praying that the plane Jacob had promised him was waiting. He reached the abandoned airfield outside Kolka, and ran onto the tarmac. He was met by the peppering of gunfire. He dove into a nearby clump of trees and waited. The engines overhead were getting louder. He looked for the plane that Jacob had promised him, finally spotting it behind a tall hedge about thirty feet away. With the pack in one hand and the rifle in the other, he crouched low and sprinted to the plane. Gunshots came again, and he zigzagged to avoid them. His rifle fell from his hand; he couldn't go back for it. He reached the plane, catching a glimpse of the eastern skyline from the corner of his eye. A faint glimmer of yellow on the horizon meant that the sun would be rising soon. He needed to hurry.

He jumped in the Cessna just as a spotlight pierced the darkness, lighting the airfield in unforgiving light. He turned the key, thankful when he heard the engine roar to life. He stared at the dials, recalling the last time he had sat at the controls of a Cessna. It was when he was a small boy, and now, years later, he could still hear his father's stern, yet kind voice. *"Check the gauges, make sure the pressure is correct, and keep that throttle in position, son."*

He focused on the instruments. Because of his father's training, he knew tricks they didn't teach in flight school; tactical maneuvers, evasive ploys...all the things he would need to elude the long reach of the Hendersons. It was as if his father – from his grave – was helping him. He felt a pang of grief as he thought of all that the man had done for him. He had been a good father; he had given Zebulun all that he could. But he was also weak, easily beaten down by a voracious wife and an even more voracious government. Zebulun tightened his jaw as he felt tears sting his cheeks. He grimaced; the tears were like poison as they trickled into his mouth and down his throat. *Viktor is gone, along with his weaknesses...now I have a new father...now I have Jacob.*

He sped down the runway and lifted to the sky, turning the plane away from the helicopters with a triumphant raising of his fist. He looked down as the shadows of dawn embraced the Baltic Sea. The gray ocean seemed quiet and still; the day had yet to begin for the ice-cold water. *Farewell, my Baltic friend.*

He outran the choppers and headed south, making sure to stay under the radar. They tried to keep up with him, but the Cessna was too fast. The first rays of sunlight shone through the window, illuminating the interior with a welcome glow. He grinned; the warm sun felt good on his cheeks...he felt at home in the plane. He continued south for another fifty miles, then turned west, careful to stay below the radar, at least until he was closer to his final stop. Jacob had told him, *"Fly south to Germany. There you will be safe."*

After about ten minutes, he looked behind him but saw nothing. No choppers, no planes; he had escaped the Henderson army. The longer he flew, the more relaxed he became. He had dodged their unmatched artillery; he had shirked their massive reach. He flinched as he thought of the brave Emek, who had risked everything to comfort a fallen soldier. Then he looked at the blood on his sleeve where the Ninja had gotten him with his knife. He cleared his throat and nodded. "I will have a scar to show my triumph over a brave, but foolish enemy."

He flew into German air space just as the sun rose over the Alps, and he smiled. *God greets me.* He gave his coordinates to a small airport outside Berlin, filled with pride as they hailed him with a hearty, *"Willkommen in Deutschland."* He replied, *"Danka,"* laughing as he felt the adrenaline race through him. He had done it.

He landed the Cessna in a small airfield outside Erkner and jumped from the plane. He walked to the terminal, the brisk morning air filling his lungs as the warm sun beat against his face. He breathed in deep, the hint of musty gentian rich in the air. He looked to the sky and said to no one in particular, "Jacob, it has begun."

End of Part I

Thank you for reading.
Please review this book. Reviews
help others find Absolutely Amazing eBooks and
inspire us to keep providing these marvelous tales.
If you would like to be put on our email list
to receive updates on new releases,
contests, and promotions, please go to
AbsolutelyAmazingEbooks.com and sign up.

About the Author

Dr. Jill Vosler is a family physician whose medical studies took her abroad to the University of Edinburgh in Scotland and on to extensive travel throughout the UK and Europe. Her love for these places has flavored her novels, along with the many years spent as a deputy coroner under the guidance of her father, who was the county coroner well into his eighties. She has a keen interest in politics and a passion for music, but most enjoys traveling the world with her husband, John, and their son and daughter.

The New
Atlantian Library

NewAtlantianLibrary.com or
AbsolutelyAmazingEbooks.com
or AA-eBooks.com

www.ingramcontent.com/pod-product-compliance
Lightning Source LLC
Chambersburg PA
CBHW071834020726
47502CB00004B/1351